OUTCLASSED
IN KUWAIT

Outclassed in Kuwait

Taleb Alrefai

Hamad bin Khalifa University Press
P O Box 5825
Doha, Qatar

www.hbkupress.com

Copyright © Taleb Alrefai, 2018
All rights reserved.

Cover photo: nullplus / Shutterstock.com

No part of this publication may be reproduced or transmitted
in any form or by any means, electronic or mechanical,
including photocopying, recording, or any information
storage or retrieval system, without prior permission
in writing from the publishers.

No responsibility for loss caused to any individual or organization
acting on or refraining from action as a result of the material in
this publication can be accepted by HBKU Press or the author.

ISBN: 978-9927119385

Qatar National Library Cataloging-in-Publication (CIP)

Rifā'ī, Ṭālib, author.

Outclassed in Kuwait / by Taleb Alrefai. – Doha : Hamad Bin Khalifa University Press , 2018.

Pages ; cm

ISBN: 978-9927-119-38-5

1. Arabic fiction – 21st century. II. Title.

PJ7860.I4 O98 2018

892.736–dc23   201826680828

To my mother Modhy Alfahad and my father Mahmoud Alrefai.

May their souls Rest In Peace.

Chapter 1

Wednesday, March 28, 2007

It was half past two in the afternoon. Exhausted, I was driving home along Morocco Highway, annoyed by the snarled traffic. My mobile rang. I didn't recognize the number.

"Hello?" I said.

"Taleb Alrefai?" a woman's soft voice asked.

"Yes," I replied.

"Good afternoon."

"And the same to you."

"This is Khalid Khalifa's office calling."

Khalid Khalifa … I recalled his pictures in the newspapers. A businessman prominent in Kuwait in particular and in the Gulf generally. I'd never met him, of course.

"Mr. Khalifa would like to speak with you," the voice informed me. "Please hold."

A mellow male voice came on the line. "Good afternoon."

"Good afternoon to you," I replied.

"I'm delighted to be speaking with a novelist and writer such as yourself."

A small amount of pride bubbled up in me. I wouldn't expect prominent businessmen to know of my writing. I thanked him.

"Mr. Alrefai, I would be honored if we could meet. Could we set a time?" he asked in a friendly tone.

"I'd be happy to." How had he gotten my mobile number? I wondered.

The traffic was beginning to flow now on Fourth Ring Road.

"Let's say at my office at eight o'clock this evening," Mr. Khalifa suggested, rather as if issuing an order.

***

"Did he say why he wants to meet you?" Shoroq, my wife, asked when I told her about the call.

"No. We agreed to meet this evening at his office in the Alraya Complex."

"Wow. That's a luxurious complex," she said.

It was half past seven already. I didn't want to be late. I stood in front of the mirror combing my hair and noticed a few gray hairs peeking through.

Shoroq was giving our young daughter, Fadia, her dinner in front of the TV in our bedroom.

"You know, sometimes I don't understand you! How can you go and meet someone without asking him what he wants from you?"

"That's the way I am," I said simply, glancing at myself in the mirror.

Shoroq got up and we embraced goodbye. I bent over to kiss my daughter, then Shoroq quickly, before splashing on some cologne and leaving the room.

"Take my car!" Shoroq's voice echoed down the stairs.

"I will, thanks!"

When I opened the front door, a pleasant March breeze brushed my face.

I would take Fourth Ring Road and then Morocco Highway towards Kuwait City, where the Alraya Complex was located. I hoped to arrive a little early; I never liked to be late.

Maybe Shoroq was right, I thought. It would have been better if I had asked him why he wanted to see me, so I could prepare myself. But whatever the reason, I would never refuse to meet someone like Khalid Khalifa.

Part of me was optimistic. Khalid was a well-known businessman, of course, so I hoped the meeting would bring good news.

When Khalid had spoken to me, he had sounded cordial enough, but still I hoped our meeting wouldn't last too long. I needed to get home as I had a lot of reading to do and I had to finish my weekly column for the newspaper.

I didn't know how long I could go on putting up with the feeling of being overloaded. I found it difficult to organize my day. I would wake up at half past five in the morning and go to bed after midnight. I was always tired and found it hard to manage my time. My work at the National Council, my domestic responsibilities, my reading and writing ... not to mention my concerns for my older daughter, Farah, who was far away in America. And, of course, the social obligations I could not escape. Reading and writing required your entire life, really.

Sometimes I thought a writer would be best off stranded on an island alone. No family or anyone else to take him away from his shelter.

About seven more minutes and I would reach the Alraya Complex. I felt a headache coming on. I wished I'd taken a Panadol before leaving.

***

After lunch, I had gone into the bedroom, switched my mobile to silent mode, and had a short nap. I had tried to guess the reason behind Khalid's request to meet with me, but I just fell asleep. In a dream, I saw myself walking in an ancient, crowded Arab market, slippery mud beneath my feet, the place abuzz with the sounds of traditional traders. I suddenly saw my mother sitting in a corner, her lap filled with small white flowers that she was handing out to passers-by in return for coins. I ran towards her to help her stand up, but she refused and looked at me curiously.

"Come, Mother," I said.

She remained silent, her face filled with curiosity.

"I am Taleb, your son. Come, Mother."

I put out my hand to her, but it hit the wooden headboard of my bed and I woke up …

***

I decided to listen to some music. I had given up listening to songs many years earlier; I preferred instrumental music. I could often be found searching out CDs of piano, clarinet, saxophone, oud, and nature and folk music.

I was happy to take Shoroq's Mercedes. My Chevrolet was old, purchased more than five years earlier. American cars begin to sag after the fifth year. I had to get rid of it, but I didn't think it would fetch more than 1,500 dinars. But that would be enough for the deposit on a new car. I wanted something small. I really liked the Mini Cooper; it felt like a unique kind of car, which was good since I was often alone in the car.

The traffic on Morocco Highway was light. The lights of the Kuwait Liberation Towers, in the heart of Kuwait City, could be seen in the distance.

I drove on as if heading to my office at the National Council for Culture, Art, and Letters. The historic Alsha'b Gate was on my left, the stoic and only remaining witness to the mud wall that once surrounded old Kuwait City. Some kind of monster had attacked the neighborhoods of the old city, gobbled up its quiet homes, and scattered the memories of its people. The old city had simply disappeared.

When Khalid Khalifa had spoken to me that afternoon, his voice had sounded welcoming. I was flattered because very few businessmen in Kuwait were interested in reading or literature. He had probably heard about one of my novels or read one of my articles in the newspaper, so he wanted to meet me, I was guessing. This might be my lucky day, I thought.

I should have called my friend Suleiman to ask about Khalid. He was also a businessman and must have known him.

Good, I would arrive a few minutes early for the meeting. I could see the Alraya Complex now. The parking lot looked a little crowded, but I'd try to find a spot near the lift.

There were few entertainment venues in Kuwait, so people enjoyed eating in restaurants or wandering in the malls and people-watching.

The arrows pointed to the lifts. Getting in, I could check how I looked. I liked mirrors in lifts. Then I reached the right floor.

A soothing calm prevailed. I asked the receptionist for Mr. Khalifa's office and he showed me the way.

"Welcome, Mr. Alrefai," a woman in her early thirties greeted me. "You look exactly like your photo in the newspaper."

I smiled. Her fair skin, short blond hair, and upper lip reminded me of Meg Ryan. The fragrance of expensive incense filled the secretary's well-furnished room.

"I'll tell Mr. Khalifa you're here."

When she stood up, I noticed her well-proportioned figure.

She has a sexy, beautiful body, I said to myself, and then suppressed the thought.

Khalid Khalifa came out of his office to greet me. "Welcome, Mr. Alrefai," he said. He was in fact more handsome than his newspaper photos would suggest. "I'm most happy to be visited by a novelist."

His tall, bulky body filled the doorway. He was wearing the Kuwaiti *dishdasha, ghutra*, and *agal*, together with shiny Bally shoes. I remembered one of my college girlfriends saying that cleanliness and the shine on a man's shoes were indicators of his character. Smiling, he put out his hand for me to shake.

"Please come in." He stepped back so I could enter his office.

I noticed an incense burner, with fragrant smoke still rising. The office was spacious, with several Persian carpets adorning the floor. On the wall behind Khalid's desk hung a large oil painting in warm colors.

Sitting down on a sofa facing me, he asked, "Tea, coffee, Perrier?"

"Just water, please."

This place reeks of wealth, I thought.

A young man in uniform entered, perhaps a Pakistani. He stood by the door waiting for Khalid's order.

"A glass of water," Khalid said, then turned to me. "We are probably the same age."

"Perhaps. I was born in 1958."

"Ah, that makes me two years older then."

I smiled.

"But if we were ever seen together, people would think I'm ten years older than you!"

"No, no. I wouldn't say so."

I noticed he was breathing heavily.

There were two identical frames on Khalid's desk. In the first, there was a black-and-white photo of Egyptian President Gamal Abdel Nasser and Sheikh Abdullah Al-Salem, former Emir of Kuwait, and in the second, a photo of himself wearing a graduation gown and holding a certificate, a short man wearing spectacles at his side.

The young man came in, carrying a glass of water.

"Will you drink coffee with me?"

"If you like, thank you."

When he stood up, the swish of his *dishdasha* stirred the sleeping incense smell.

"Coffee *dallah*," he said to his secretary. Then returning to his seat, he added, "I'll tell you what's on my mind. I would like you to write a novel about me."

He said it as if asking a salesman for a product and expecting the salesman to bring it to him from stock. I was taken aback by the request and took a sip of water.

"A novel?"

"Yes."

"I don't know if I could really write such a novel."

He pulled himself up straight and stared at me. There was something mysterious about his request.

"I've never written a biographical novel," I added. "Maybe you mean a straight biography documenting your life?"

"No, a novel," he replied. So he knew the difference between a novel and a work of non-fiction. I would never have expected a businessman to ask me to write a biographical novel.

"I'm an enthusiastic reader and passionate about novels, you see. I want you to write a novel about me just like the novels you've written before."

I listened carefully to every word he said.

The dream about my mother handing out flowers to passers-by in return for charity came back to me. I thought of myself giving out novels to all comers.

"I'll tell you the story of my life and you'll write it as a novel. You will use my real name and you'll take credit as the author," he said.

The idea surprised me, and the easy way he said it surprised me even more. He said it as if the novel could be written in one sitting.

"Perhaps you've read some of my work? I write about distinctive worlds," I said.

"What kind of worlds?" he asked, focusing closely on my face.

"Some of my writing depicts Kuwaiti people as troubled; some of it deals with the sufferings of immigrant workers in Kuwait."

"Why do you write about those people?" he asked. The way he asked the question irritated me.

"Because I'm one of them and I share their suffering."

I had second thoughts about my own remark. My life was not that bad.

The two of us fell silent. Then he looked at me and continued. "Poor people live in suffering all the time." There was a hint of distress in his tone. "Who said that businessmen are happy all the time and free from worry?"

"No one is free from worry, of course," I agreed. Some businessmen believed they could buy anything, I thought to myself.

"Don't make a hasty decision," he said in a friendly tone. "Please, give yourself time to think about it."

I remained silent, considering him, his confidence, his influence, his friendly voice, and the smell of incense around him. Don't forget his money, a part of me said.

I felt that everything in the office was focusing on me – the silence, the furniture, the colors of the painting, His Highness

Sheikh Abdullah Al-Salem, Khalid's breathing, the smell of incense, the glass of water ...

"Have you ever read any of my novels or short stories?" I asked.

"I've read three of your novels, yes, and I follow your weekly newspaper column."

His quick reply made me feel that he was hiding something.

"My daughter, Mai, has read most of your works. She has a large room full of books and she loves to read."

"That's wonderful. How old is she?"

A young man holding a coffee *dallah* entered the room. At his side, another young man brought in a tray with a golden dish filled with dates.

Khalid urged me to try them. "Our coffee is good and the dates are excellent."

The young man bent over in front of me and proffered a small coffee cup. The scent of cardamom hit me from the cup. I took a date, placed it in my mouth, and sipped the bitter coffee before shaking the cup to indicate I'd had enough.

"Mai's in her late twenties," Khalid explained. "It was she who recommended you. She said your novels deal courageously with contemporary issues in Kuwaiti society and that you include autobiographical details in them."

The way he spoke about his daughter reminded me of my daughter Farah. I was strangely possessed by a desire to see his daughter.

"Mai will be very happy if you accept my proposal." There's a woman behind this story, I thought.

I need time to think, I told myself.

"Mai is my eldest daughter and the closest to my heart."

"I also have a special relationship with my older daughter," I said.

"How old is she?"

"Twenty-three."

"Where does she work?"

"She's doing a master's degree in journalism in the States."

"Kuwait is amazing! The Ministry of Education sends our daughters to study at universities across the world while members of parliament protest against the Minister of Education not wearing the veil!"

He talked to me as if we were friends. His behavior confused me. I didn't know how to build a relationship with someone I'd only just met. I was normally taciturn, withdrawn within myself.

"I'm still waiting for your response," he said.

I felt I had to be firm and honest. I couldn't write a novel about him. Who was he that I should write a novel about him? I didn't want to be aggressive, though, so I said, "I cannot reply just yet. Biographies show the chronological progression of a person's character. I think any good journalist could help you write your life story."

"I called you because I want you personally to write my life story in the form of a novel." What a dilemma, I thought.

"This would be a sizable project. It could take a year, and my work at the National Council consumes all my time. Plus, I've never written a biography."

"I think you have. You wrote a book about the writer Abdul Razzaq Albaseer, didn't you?"

He seemed to know a lot about me.

"Abdul Razzaq Albaseer is a writer of the Kuwaiti enlightenment," I said, "and I wrote a book about him, not a novel. It was an appreciation of his role as a cultural pioneer."

Khalid looked at me.

"To write a novel about you, that's a completely a different story. Biographies document people's lives, while novels create an exciting imaginary life."

He continued looking at me quietly.

"If I wrote a novel about you, could I write whatever I wanted?" I asked.

"We would have to first agree on the basic principle and then go into the details."

Something in his decisive reply worried me.

"Why do you want me specifically to write about you?"

"As I told you, my daughter ... How about I answer all of your questions after we make an agreement?"

"Whether I agree to this or not depends on your answers, though." I realized I was speaking as if we already had an agreement in principle. In order to escape any firm commitment, I said, "Let's fix a date for another meeting and we'll see."

"When?"

"Are you in a hurry?"

"Everyone is nowadays. Mai and I have already spent more than five months discussing the idea. Shall we meet at the beginning of next week?"

"Yes, OK."

Standing up, he said, "It's been a pleasure to meet you." He put out his hand for me to shake. "I hope you will agree to write my novel. Nothing is given for free, of course. You will be well paid." Those are the magic words! I said to myself.

The dream about my mother came back to me again. Khalid's eyes met mine. Think about it! He is a millionaire! said a voice in the back of my head.

"We'll see. Well, goodbye for now."

I walked away, my mind confused. What secret lurked behind this offer? A millionaire wanted to entertain himself by writing his life's story? Or maybe there was something else, something more complicated going on.

Now, where had I parked my car?

Chapter 2

Wednesday, March 28, 2007

The moment I left Khalid's office, I decided that a visit to my friend Suleiman and his wife Samar was in order. Suleiman was a businessman who owned numerous companies and Samar was a bank manager. They certainly knew Khalid, so they might be able to help me decide what to do. I thought I might also call my friend the novelist Ismail Fahad Ismail to ask his opinion, too.

I had serious reservations. This wasn't really my way of writing – to be employed by a businessman to write what he wanted me to write.

My phone had been on silent mode during the meeting but I saw that Shoroq had called me three times.

I reached my car.

It had never crossed my mind that I would write a novel about a businessman and be paid by him.

It would mark a sharp departure from my previous practice, and other writers might well criticize me if I wrote for money.

I had never heard of an Arab writer producing a novel on demand for a private client. Kuwaiti society is small and many people would probably know Khalid Khalifa's life story. Yet he wanted this biographical novel to be written by me. And he wanted to use my name. At the same time, I'd been looking for a new idea for my next writing project for a year. Writing about Khalid did sound original.

I drove home, mulling things over.

I opened the door to silence, and climbed the stairs to the first floor.

"Good evening," I said.

Shoroq was sitting waiting for me in front of the TV in the lounge.

She got up to greet me. "Hi. I was just about to go check on Fadia."

I followed her to go and get changed. Once in our bedroom, I took off my jacket and tie and then put my shoes in their place while Shoroq checked on Fadia.

I walked over and watched my little girl stir in her slumber. I wondered what she was dreaming about. I smiled and pushed back a small lock of her hair.

Having tucked her in, Shoroq looked at me.

"So, what did Mr. Khalid want from you?"

"He wants me to write a novel about him."

An astonished look flashed in her eyes.

"You want me to prepare your dinner?" she asked.

"Only fruit for me," I replied.

***

Wearing pajamas and eyeglasses, Shoroq was watching over Fadia as she slept, waiting for me in our favorite spot in front of the small bedroom TV. I slumped down next to her, bringing my bad mood with me. Khalid's offer was running through my head. I didn't know what to say.

"Khalid Khalifa asked me to write a novel about him," I repeated.

For a moment or two, her face remained expressionless. "What did you tell him?"

"Nothing. He caught me by surprise."

"How was the meeting? Did you discuss any details?" she asked.

"We didn't discuss any details. Since he surprised me with the idea, I didn't know what to say, so we agreed to meet again."

"What are you going to tell him?"

"That I can't write about him."

When a new idea started running through my head, I wanted to be alone. For me, silence was an opportunity to think more clearly and make better decisions.

"I'm not going to write this novel," I said. "Let him look for another writer to make him look good." I thought to myself: I'm sure there are many others waiting for an opportunity like this.

"You look upset. Why?" asked Shoroq.

I tried to recall details of our meeting. "I feel that something in his words rather insulted me."

"If you don't want to write about him, just make your apologies and that'll be the end of it."

She made it sound so easy. Although the TV volume was low, I wished she would switch it off. But she liked the background sound.

"He wants me to write a biographical novel about his life. But I can't imagine myself receiving instructions from a businessman dictating to me what to write. A novelist is more important and more long-lasting than any businessman." Shoroq looked at me. "I don't really know why the meeting bothered me. You know that in the Arab world no writer has ever taken money to write a biographical novel about a businessman. The idea is just unacceptable! It goes against my convictions. I've built up a relationship of trust with my readers and I want to keep it respectable. I don't like the idea of selling myself to him, or to anyone. I can just imagine what Kuwaiti readers will say: Taleb Alrefai sold his principles and wrote a novel for money!"

"Why don't you give yourself a chance to think about it calmly?" Shoroq suggested.

"I'm not a good fit for this. I'll turn down his offer and let him look for another writer."

"Don't make a hasty decision. Give yourself a little time and think it over calmly."

"OK."

We both looked at the images flashing across the TV screen.

"It would be possible to imagine the life of a nationally known businessman and write about him, but to write about a millionaire only because he desires it, that's another thing."

"Is it the idea you're rejecting? Or is it that you're afraid of writing about a real businessman?" Shoroq asked.

I looked at her. "I don't know," I admitted.

Fadia slept while the film on the TV continued. Peace on one side of the room, frantic images on the other.

"How will I ever find out about the hidden aspects of his life?" I said. "Will he allow me to recreate his character as I wish? Actually, I thought about dropping in on Suleiman and Ismael – you know, to get their opinions."

"Mmm. You should call them, yes. For quite a while now you've been looking for an idea for a new novel."

I was beginning to see that it was an original idea and might possibly work.

"Look at it from a different angle," said Shoroq. "Perhaps it's a good thing that a millionaire thinks about writing his biography in the form of a novel. What's wrong with that?"

"Writing represents freedom. I can't simply write to order. Writing a novel for Khalid means a contract, an obligation."

"So?"

A quiet moment passed between us.

I could see some merit in Shoroq's argument, but I wasn't convinced.

"There's a big difference between when a novelist chooses to write the biography of a businessman as he pleases and when a businessman dictates to a novelist what he wants to be written about him," I said.

"So what will he give you in return?" Shoroq asked, switching tack.

"He said it would be a generous amount."

"How much?"

"We didn't discuss a figure."

"What's a generous amount to a millionaire, do you think?"

I paused and ran my hand through my hair. It might have been graying, but I still had plenty of it. "I don't know," I said.

Our eyes met and she said with a laugh, "If he says he's going to give you a generous amount, I'm sure it'll be acceptable!"

"Right," I said, just to go along with her.

"Look, we're in debt. Our house is mortgaged to the bank and the monthly installments eat up our salaries. We might be able to pay off part of our mortgage …"

Our talk had suddenly taken a different turn, and become more intense.

"Are you serious?"

"Yes," she said. "The man is a millionaire and he values money differently from us. And he's the one who called you, don't forget."

"His daughter suggested my name to him."

Something flashed in Shoroq's look. "Oh? His daughter?"

"I don't know her, but he said she's a reader. She has a small library and she's read all my books apparently."

"He didn't say that she's one of your 'admirers'?" she asked in a sarcastic tone.

"No, he didn't say that," I replied, my tone mirroring hers.

"Is the millionaire's daughter going to be a part of the novel, too?" Shoroq asked. Ah, a woman's sense of jealousy, I thought.

I sensed an acrimonious turn in the conversation. "He asked me to write a novel about him," I said. "He told me no more about her than that he has a special relationship with her."

"Did you ask about her age?"

"Why are you asking me this?"

"Because …"

It was almost eleven o'clock. I felt heavy-hearted and unable to concentrate. And I had a headache, on top of my back pain. I got up.

"I'm tired. I'm going to bed."

Shoroq quickly got up, too. "Sorry. Did I upset you?"

"It doesn't matter. It's my back. It's been hurting me most of the day." Before I could say anything more, she hugged me.

"I love you. I still feel jealous sometimes." She led me over to the couch. "Do you want a Panadol?"

"No, I want to sleep."

She took my hand and said, "You have to think about this in a different way."

"The offer surprised me. And writing any novel is a big undertaking," I insisted.

"I know, but this is something different. It's a prepaid novel."

"But it will still be a novel with my name on it. Think about my friends, especially other Arab writers. They'll say, 'Shame on you, Taleb!' I never heard of any Arab writer taking money to write a novel on demand."

"Whatever your friends believe, that's up to them."

"Accepting the principle of writing a novel for money sets a new precedent," I said, not with complete conviction.

"What about our financial problems? My love, please forget about those wretched communist principles you believe in this one time. The world has changed."

"I'm talking about my own principles."

"Please, let's not throw away this chance. Think carefully. When will you see him again?"

"Saturday."

She nudged me playfully. "Come on, you have to accept the offer. It's tempting!"

I smiled at her.

"You'll get a lot of money. J.K. Rowling became a millionaire from her Harry Potter novels."

I laughed. "That happened in Britain, not here in Kuwait or in any Arab country."

"People are trading in everything. We live in a crazy consumer society where culture has become a commodity, and your trade is writing novels."

"So, in your opinion, what would be an appropriate amount?" I asked her jokingly.

"Ah, you know better than me. You know how much an Arab novelist gets when publishing a novel, don't you?"

I knew the right answer was nothing.

She stayed silent, looking at me.

"You know what the reality is," I said. "Many Arab novelists pay publishers to see their books published and get no more than a thousand copies printed."

"I don't want the boring details. Tell me, how much does an Arab novelist make from a successful novel?"

"1,000 U.S. dollars – if he's lucky."

"Let's say, 3,000 or 6,000 dollars, then. That's less than 2,000 Kuwaiti dinars. So you should ask for 10,000 dinars."

She turned off the TV and an empty silence spread through the house. Suddenly she said, "Ask for 20,000 dinars."

Her idea caught me off guard. But still, I would feel like a mercenary the moment I stood in front of Khalid asking him for money.

"Look, the man is a millionaire, right? He called you and promised to give you a generous amount of money for writing the novel. Why don't you ask for 50,000?"

I smiled. "Let's go to sleep now," I said. "If we stay up any longer, you'll raise the price to 100,000!"

"So what? My father is a businessman and I look at things differently."

For a few moments, I thought how 100,000 dinars would pay off a large part of our mortgage and spare me those monthly installments that consumed most of my salary.

"Please remember that we don't live on a desert island," Shoroq said. "We only live one life. And I'm sick of trying so hard to make ends meet. We work every month to pay our debts and loans. I need some money. *You* don't go to receptions, to parties, meet with women, and see their diamonds, watches, bags, expensive dresses, and shoes. I'm no less than anyone else!"

"There's no connection between all of this and writing a novel," I interrupted, surprised at her admission.

"If writing this will bring us some money, I don't see why you can't accept doing it."

"I can't write a novel like this," I said, though something inside me said I might consider being less obstinate.

I could see the disappointment in Shoroq's eyes. "I don't know. Let's leave this till later, OK?" I said in a tired voice. There was still that sad look in her eyes. "I'll be seeing him on Saturday evening. I'll ask for 50,000, OK?" I added.

"Ask for more."

"More than 50,000?"

"50,000 is nothing for a millionaire. Start with 100,000 dinars and gradually go down to 90, 80 if you need to. Try to get as much as you can. 100,000 dinars would solve a lot of our problems."

Shoroq fell silent. I thought about our difficult financial situation – the bank loans, Fadia's school fees, our daily expenses. Sometimes we were forced to use our Visa credit card after the first week of the month. Shoroq once told me that girls came to university wearing diamonds and expensive bags from brands such as Louis Vuitton, Christian Dior, and Hermes. Most of those bags are fake, by the way, I had said to myself.

"The streets of Kuwait are full of Lexus, Mercedes, and Porsche cars," Shoroq continued. "I don't know where people get all their money! You talk about your Arab writer friends, then let them know the truth about Kuwaitis. Let them know that the conditions we live in are not like they seem from the outside. This consumer society makes us live to pay our monthly installments! And besides, who would tell your friends you've been paid to write this novel?" There's more gossip among writers than you think, I said to myself.

"Maybe I'll become another person when I write this novel," I said.

"How long would it take you to complete?"

"I don't know, maybe a year or so. He told me he had read my three novels."

"What did he think of them?"

"Well, he didn't actually tell me. He only said he follows my newspaper columns." To change the subject, I said, "I feel like I'm on Candid Camera."

Shoroq looked confused. "Might this all be some kind of trick?"

I wondered about that. "Anything is possible, I suppose."

"But you recognized the man."

"Yes, the handsome millionaire whose picture fills the business pages."

"What if he set you up with one of your friends in TV or the media?"

"Then this would be a very silly joke."

Shoroq nodded. "So we have to be careful, then."

I rose, but before I stepped into the bathroom, she barged past me.

"Can't wait, sorry!"

I thought to myself how 100,000 dinars was a large amount of money. I told myself to think about it. I knew it bothered me, but still.

The idea ran through my head and I wondered what awaited me.

Chapter 3

Saturday, March 31, 2007

It was twenty minutes to eight. I had just come out of the office of Ismail Fahad, one of my best friends. I needed less than ten minutes to reach Khalid's office. Ismail had written more than thirty novels, and so I was keen to hear his opinion.

When I told him about Khalid's offer, he quietly responded, "Why not? Writing a biographical novel is an interesting approach."

"It is, but the man wants a novel for his own satisfaction."

"Yes, but you are the one who'll actually write it. Let him ask for everything he wants and then you write it in your own language and style. It'll be a new experience for you. He's a millionaire and he promised you good money, so go ahead."

"If a businessman asked you to write about him, would you agree?"

"Of course I would," he responded immediately, as if he had been expecting my question. He looked at me. "I'll be waiting for your new novel."

I recognized the encouraging tone, so I said simply, "I'll do what I can."

I had intended to ask him whether he thought it was acceptable to write a novel on demand, and how other Arab writers, critics, and readers might regard this, but his clarity helped me to feel that the matter was settled. He hadn't expressed any reservations.

***

The Salhiya area is in the center of Kuwait City. At night, it is crowded with drivers, laborers, and maids – Filipinos, Indians, and Pakistanis, who together give the place a special identity. There was a traffic jam at the roundabout, so I took Alsoor Street.

You'll need to be careful, I thought. This would be very much a new adventure.

I smiled.

I made a turn into the Alraya Complex.

That morning Khalid's secretary, Meg Ryan, had reminded me of the meeting with Khalid and said he would be waiting for me at eight o'clock. I parked my car. It was seven minutes to eight, so I was a little early, good.

Meg Ryan smiled when she saw me and told me that Mr. Khalifa was about to arrive. She is sexy, I thought, though I was embarrassed at the thought.

The telephone rang and she answered. "Yes, he's arrived. Mr. Khalifa apologizes for the delay. He'll be here in five minutes."

"I arrived a little early," I said. "I don't know your name," I added, trying to be friendly.

"My name is Miriam," she replied. "I'm from Lebanon."

"Did anyone ever tell you that you look like the actress Meg Ryan?" I continued.

"Actually, my friends call me Meg."

I smiled at her. "I like her movies, actually."

She suddenly switched to a more official tone. "What would you like to drink?"

"Nothing, thank you."

I remembered Farah's joy the previous day when she said, "You've become a famous writer and now rich people are running after you to write novels about them!"

My relationship with Farah had changed since she left to study. She had suddenly moved from the warmth, safety, and cosseting of family life to an independent life in America. She had rented an apartment and now lived a quiet and lonely life there. With no relatives nearby, she had been transformed into another girl and forced me to treat her differently. I had always thought and worried about her before, but her moving away to study had made me more anxious. And I missed her so much, even though we talked every day on the Internet, sometimes even more often.

***

Shoroq and I had visited Suleiman and Samar the day before. Samar sat chatting with Shoroq about her troubles trying to get pregnant. She was having another IVF, which she desperately hoped would succeed this time.

"I know Khalid Khalifa," Suleiman said. "He's a decent man and has a good reputation. He runs successful companies and is one of the most famous businessmen in Kuwait. And he's the husband of the multimillionaire Awatef Al-Abdullatif too."

"I know who she is but I didn't know she was Khalid's wife," I said.

"Khalid comes from a poor family, but the rich Abdullatif family made him a big name after he married their daughter." Suleiman paused a few seconds before adding, "It's generally known that Khalid and his wife are separated now." I wonder how happy the multimillionaire woman will be when you write a novel about her husband, I said to myself.

Last year I was in Dubai for a short visit when I had a mysterious urge to call and check on Fadia. Somehow I had a vision of my little girl with a cut on a finger of her left hand. I could see her crying at the sight of blood. When I phoned home, I heard Fadia crying in the background.

"Fadia just cut her finger with a sharp knife," Shoroq explained.

"Where?"

"The index finger on her left hand."

As always, I had kept my secret insight to myself.

Yesterday, after breakfast, I went to my office on the ground floor to archive my articles as I usually did on Fridays. The idea of writing the novel for Khalid Khalifa was worrying me. I knew I had to think it over carefully as it would take many people by surprise. I had written stories exposing the misery and deaths of foreign laborers in Kuwait and stories condemning outdated social practices. And now I was preparing to write a novel glorifying a millionaire.

I will not glorify anyone, I had said to myself. I'll write it because I need the money to pay off my debts.

I thought about it and out of nowhere the question came to me: Why did I insist on living in poverty?

***

"I'm so sorry," I heard Khalid say as he approached. "I had a doctor's appointment," he added, shaking my hand. It was clear he had some difficulty breathing.

"I hope everything is OK?"

He ignored my question and took me into his office. A strong smell of incense and aromatic wood came with him. He was well dressed again. We entered his office, and without thinking, I went to the same seat I had sat in the last time.

"Again, I'm sorry for my tardiness. I'm usually punctual. I don't like delays."

"It's fine, Mr. Khalifa."

"Driving in Kuwait is enough to make anyone crazy!"

The coffee boy came in carrying the incense burner.

Khalid told the boy to put it down on the table in front of me.

"What can I offer you to drink?"

"Water, please."

"Bring us tea and water." He turned to me. "I recommend our mint tea."

"As you like."

The white smoke of the incense rose. Ten grams of this incense might well cost over 100 dinars, I thought, probably more than the entire monthly salary of the coffee boy. I wondered why Mr. Khalifa burned his money to make white smoke. The answer was obvious: Because he wanted to say to everyone, "Look, I'm a millionaire!"

"So, have you decided?" Khalid asked me.

"I'd be lying if I said no and also if I said yes."

"I see. I think that means you agree but you don't want to say it openly," he said with a smile.

While listening to him, my eye rested on his diamond-studded pen. I remembered what Suleiman had told me. "Mr. Khalifa is a cultured, modern-thinking man and is known for his passion for elegance. He was one of the most handsome students in Kuwait University in the seventies, you know. The girls all hovered around him."

"I want you to write a novel about my life," Khalid said, making me focus again on the conversation. "But it has to stay away from my family life. I want you to focus on my experiences in business. This will be a novel about a Kuwaiti businessman."

"For me, writing a novel is like going to sea in a fishing boat. I might return with a catch of fish, or I might get lost, or run into a storm, and look for a lifeline."

Khalid didn't seem to know what to make of my idea. The tea boy's entrance was timely.

"Put it here," Khalid told him. "As I told you, I don't really understand the process of writing, but I want you to write a novel telling the true story of my life." His voice turned serious. "I made sure to choose a novelist who knows and understands the forces at play in Kuwaiti society."

I was touched by this. He was silent for a few seconds as if recalling something.

"Novelists have a special relationship with words, I know. They have a power. They know how to mold words into sentences so they say things in a way we might not consciously be aware of."

What he said suggested a certain literary sensibility.

"Have you ever written anything yourself?" I asked.

He smiled. "I wish, but no."

Our eyes met. A faint smile appeared on his face.

"My daughter Mai and I planned this novel. You and I will meet six or seven times. At each meeting, I'll talk about one stage in my life and my work. You'll collect all the necessary information and then you'll write the novel."

He stopped to catch his breath and make sure he had my attention, then added, "You have to remember always that this is a novel about my work – not about my family."

I noticed that he was already dictating his instructions.

When I smiled, Khalid asked me why.

"Because you and Mai have planned a novel that I will actually write."

He looked puzzled.

"If I write the novel, then it must be me who shapes your character and your personality," I said.

"There's no need to make it complicated. In the end, this will just be something small, not a major work. You'll write it and show it to Mai and me for approval before you publish it."

I didn't like his tone. I looked up at him and asked, "Why don't you write your own story?"

After a few moments of silence, Khalid finally said, "If I could write, I wouldn't let anybody else write on my behalf." The tone was sharper now.

"What if you don't like my writing style?" I asked him.

"Then you'll rewrite it."

My heart sank. "What if I can't?"

"Please, I hate to start any project with pessimism."

The way he spoke amazed me, so clearly did it reflect the reality that he would be the master and I would be an employee under his command.

"We can agree on the principle of the writing but this can't be a commercial project," I said.

"Why not?"

"In the Arab world, the market for books is limited. There's no wide reading audience, since the majority don't read."

"Let's concentrate on our project," he interrupted calmly. "When an author writes his own novel, of course he will do it as he pleases, but writing a commissioned novel means he's obliged to comply with his agreement with the other party." He was short of breath again.

"Writing a novel on request is a new experience for me."

"We'll go through this experience together."

The charcoal in the incense burner was dying down and the air around us was a little clearer.

"I agreed with Mai that she could attend our meeting today."

That piqued my interest but suddenly I realized that Khalid had yet to mention anything about payment.

Perhaps I could make a deal with him to write his story without putting my name on it as the author, I thought.

Everything was quiet in the room again.

"If we agree on this contract, when would you be ready to start writing?" he asked.

"How long do you think we'd need to complete the novel?"

"I don't know exactly, but I expect our meetings and the writing would take around six months," Khalid said with confidence.

I looked at Khalid and tried to imagine my relationship with him when he became the protagonist of my novel. I had never thought I'd find myself in this kind of situation.

"Writing is an adventure. Have you ever made a deal without knowing where it would lead you?" I asked Khalid.

"Every day I make dozens of transactions on the stock market."

"You make deals on the stock market without being sure of the profit?"

"Of course. If I waited to be sure of the profit on all the deals, I'd never have had any success or made any money! A dealer without a spirit of adventure misses a lot. Being adventurous might even be the most important characteristic of a dealer!" He looked at me as if asking me to concentrate on his words. "I don't know about writing but you say writing is an adventure."

I nodded. "A great adventure that might even take up the writer's whole life."

"Nothing makes life worth living more so than our eagerness to live it."

His words touched me. I thought a life of eagerness was a real life, and that without it life could become a heavy burden. I heard a tap on the door.

"Come in," Khalid said.

The door opened and a short young woman came in, wearing jeans and a green T-shirt, with a leather bag hanging from her shoulder. She reminded me of Farah.

"Hi, Mai," Khalid said with pleasure. "This here is the core of my very heart," he said to me.

The girl smiled bashfully. I got up to shake hands.

"I'm Taleb Alrefai."

"Yes, I know you from your writing and your photos in the newspapers."

"It's nice to meet you."

"You too, Mr. Alrefai." She turned to her father. "How was your meeting with the doctor?" she asked him in a hushed voice.

"Good, everything is excellent."

"Sure? You aren't hiding anything from me?"

"Daddy doesn't like to talk about his illness," she said, turning to me. "And sometimes he hides the truth."

I smiled at her. I noticed Khalid's irregular breathing. He got up suddenly and ordered his secretary to bring more incense.

When he sat down again, he told me, "I love the smell of incense. I feel it helps me think. When I'm facing a difficult decision, for example, I need incense."

"Are you facing a difficult decision now?" I asked.

"For months I've been trying to persuade him to agree to this," Mai answered.

I saw something of her father in her face when she spoke. She looked much younger than her age. She was short but with a well-proportioned body. Her dark brownish hair fell to her shoulders. She had small eyes and lovely, sexy lips. Her simple appearance would never suggest she was the daughter of a millionaire.

"My father deserves to have a novel written about him."

"Every girl admires her father," I joked with her.

She looked at her father, then said with a smile, "My dad's life story will make for a good novel."

"Well, I don't really know anything about Mr. Khalifa's life."

"Once you agree to do the writing, you'll find out everything." Switching to a gentler tone, she added, "Are you going to write the novel?"

I didn't answer.

She smiled and said, "Silence is a sign of consent." She looked at her father. "It seems that Mr. Alrefai is going to agree."

"I didn't say anything," I said.

But Mai did, I thought.

"Congratulations," Khalid said.

"Thanks," was my meek reply.

"Mai will arrange the contract terms with you and I will sign it and arrange times for us to sit down together." You've gotten yourself into an embarrassing position here, I thought to myself. I hadn't actually agreed to anything. But then I remembered my debts and endless financial commitments. Everything came back to me: Shoroq's words, Farah's hope, Suleiman's praise, and Ismail's approval. I wanted to abandon the idea, but something inside me prevented me. I felt a twinge of pain in my back.

"Could we postpone talking about the details of the contract to another time?" I asked Mai. "My back is hurting me and I can't sit for very long in the same position, you see."

"Come, sit here," said Khalid, pointing to a chair in front of his desk. "Let's at least agree on the payment before you leave. Then Mai can finish up everything else."

I felt out of place, caught in something beyond my control. I realized I was about to make a commitment to write a novel that I had no idea how to write.

"What do you think of 24,000 dinars? That's 2,000 dinars every month for a year," said Khalid.

I had no idea how to negotiate in financial matters, so I decided it was best to keep silent.

"A ten percent bonus on completion will increase the fee to 26,000 dinars," Khalid added.

He's reeling off these numbers like he calculated them all before, I said to myself, but you came for 100,000, don't forget. Yes. I could picture Shoroq's face very clearly. Her hopes …

Mai came to sit opposite me. I sat there in silence.

"Mr. Alrefai, how much were you thinking of?" she asked.

"I hadn't thought of an amount, actually. I've never been through a deal like this."

"Well, Dad proposed 26,000 dinars, but because I'm in love with your writing I will add another 10,000." She smiled at me, looked at her father, and said, "Let's just say 40,000, shall we?"

I was confused. Both of them were waiting for my answer and I didn't know whether to agree or ask for more. I had the impression that Mai and her father had already agreed on the amount and perhaps this was all a bit of an act to convince me.

Suleiman had told me Khalid was a generous man, so out of nowhere I blurted out, "Perhaps we should raise the amount?"

"How much?" Khalid asked me in a serious tone.

"100,000," I said.

"Agreed," he said as if he had decided beforehand. "But you

will have to finish writing the novel within one year from the date of signing the contract."

My heart raced.

For a moment I thought of seeking more in recognition of the time constraint, but the moment passed when Mai jumped in.

"Congratulations," she said to her father with a sweet smile. "It will be a very special novel," she said to me. "Tomorrow, I'll arrange the contract with the lawyer and prepare the advance."

"And the day after tomorrow, we will sign it," Khalid added cheerfully. "I would be pleased to invite you and your family to a small reception on the occasion of signing the contract."

I didn't really know what to say. Everything was new and confusing to me.

"I hope the terms of the contract remain confidential between us," Khalid added, serious again. When I didn't immediately answer, he raised his eyebrows.

"Of course!" I blurted out.

"Mai and I will not tell anyone but we'll celebrate with you when the novel is published, of course." 100,000 Kuwaiti dinars was more than 360,000 U.S. dollars, I thought. Perhaps this would be the most expensive Arab novel ever! I thought of the readership for this: all of Khalid's friends, traders, and businessmen ...

I would use the money to pay off my mortgage and bank loan – that was all I could think about. I felt overwhelmed and needed to leave.

"Let's be clear on this: the total period of the contract will be one year, starting from the date of signature," Khalid said. His sharp tone frightened me somewhat.

"What if I'm delayed?" I asked. "Creative writing isn't

something fixed and finite. Sometimes the writer gets stuck on a word or a sentence and can't write anything."

"We have to agree on a specific period of time," he replied.

"What if you fall behind schedule telling me your story?"

"I won't. I'll tell you my story faster than you can imagine."

"But suppose you're delayed for some reason. How long should I wait?"

He looked at me and said in a serious tone, "I will not fall behind." He turned to Mai. "Make the contract period a year. I'll tell my story within six months and Mr. Alrefai will finish the writing over the following six months." He paused for a few seconds to catch his breath. "And write a second paragraph noting that if I fail to tell my story within six months, for any reason, Mr. Alrefai has the right to receive full payment."

He turned back to me. "I think that's fair enough?"

I smiled, even though I didn't really like the way he was speaking. I could feel the twinge in my back.

"Tomorrow Mai will send you a copy of the contract and a check for the first installment."

Well that's that, I thought, but not with great joy.

"We'll decide on our first meeting very soon," Khalid said, speaking more slowly now. "I'll tell my wife about the contract before we begin. Her response might have an impact on how the book is written."

I stood up. "Well, I need to leave – if we're finished, of course," I said.

"Of course."

Khalid stood to say goodbye.

I hurried out and felt anxious as I made my way to my car. I wondered if I had made an awful mistake by promising to finish his novel in six months.

Chapter 4

Tuesday, April 10, 2007

I'd been good friends with the lawyer and writer Mohammed Massaad Alsaleh since the mid-seventies. He was the editor-in-chief of *Alwatan* newspaper, and I was a new writer publishing my short stories in its cultural pages. When he moved to write in *Alqabas*, I moved with him to write in the same newspaper.

After I received a copy of the contract from Khalid's office, I visited Mohammed. He welcomed me with his usual friendly smile. We sat together for a while before he asked me what he could do for me.

"Do you know Mr. Khalid Khalifa?" I asked him.

"Of course. The man is well known in the business world."

"He wants me to write a novel based on his life."

I waited for a comment but he didn't say anything.

"A novel about his work as a businessman, using his real name," I added.

"I see. And how can I help?"

"We're signing a contract – it's a commissioned novel, you see – and I wanted to get a legal opinion."

"Paid in advance?"

"In installments, yes."

"Well, there's nothing in Kuwaiti law that prohibits a writer from writing the biography of someone else. I haven't actually ever been involved in this kind of contract before, but the legal principle says, '*pacta sunt servanda.*' That is, the man has asked you for a service – he wants you to write his biography – and you as a writer can provide this service and get your fees in return."

I had always been impressed by this man's composure and clear thinking.

"It's important to state the fees and duration of the contract and the nature of the story you're going to write, though. And it should not affect the reputation or the interests of other people," he continued.

I chatted with him for nearly half an hour. "Khalid Khalifa has an excellent reputation in the market," he said. "He has extensive business activities and he's an important market analyst." He smiled. "And the man is not only a millionaire himself but also the husband of a multimillionaire."

I could see that his story might be interesting after all.

I would have liked to stay longer but after a time Mohammed got up and told me that regrettably he had another meeting.

"I hope your writing is successful," he wished me as he said goodbye.

I left his office in a good mood. He had encouraged me and given me some impetus.

When I first started out, I believed in the power of writing. I thought it could change the consciousness of society. Journalism and editorial pieces affected those who read them, but they only ever reached a limited audience. I wanted to write fiction – realistic fiction with social commentary. And, with the folly of the young, I also just wanted to be a famous writer. A celebrity – with girls, of course. It was not very long before I discovered that the path was much harder than I had thought and that there was no celebrity and no girls.

The moment I received a copy of the contract, and the first payment – for the amount of 20,000 dinars – all I thought was: Money talks.

***

It was a quarter to nine in the evening and I was on my way to Khalid's house. Our first and second meetings had taken place in his office. Tonight I would visit him in his home. My novel's protagonist – for that was how I now had to think of him, already with an emerging backstory – had given me his home address in the Abdulla Alsalem area, one of the richest neighborhoods in Kuwait. And I had his mobile number now, just in case I lost the address or had problems finding the place.

I arrived at the house. One of his drivers – or perhaps a general servant, I didn't know exactly – was waiting for me.

"Good evening, sir," the young Indian man said. "You are Mr. Alrefai?"

"I am, yes."

"Follow me, please."

He led me through the main door and we walked down a small corridor that smelled of flowers.

"Welcome," said Khalid, who was waiting for me near the entrance, wearing a *dishdasha*, his head uncovered. He shook my hand warmly and led the way. The smell of incense grew stronger as we walked through a wide lounge area. A luxury crystal chandelier hung from the ceiling. There were many little alcoves with various ornaments, beautiful silk carpets on the floor, Persian no doubt, and many paintings on the walls. We went through a dining room that had at least twenty seats.

A strange feeling came over me. I had entered the home of my novel's protagonist.

How am I going to change him into a character in a novel? I thought.

My mind was quickly taking in the surroundings, painting a picture of the man, the character, from the way his house was decorated.

"Come, let's sit in my favorite place," said Khalid, interrupting my train of thought. He led me through a smaller door into a room with a small office. White wooden shelves, full of books and photos, covered most of the walls – more character-building and backstory, I thought. We sat on two chairs next to each other.

"What would you like to drink?"

"Lemon juice, please."

"With mint?"

"Yes, that would be good, thank you."

"Lemon juice with mint," Khalid ordered the Filipina girl who had come to stand at the door.

"This is the smallest room in the house," Khalid said, turning to me. "Mai turned it into a small personal library and decorated it with pictures of the family."

"The room isn't really small, though," I said.

He smiled.

His tone was different from his tone in the office. He looked friendlier and calmer, too. And perhaps also younger without his head covered. For some reason, I had imagined him as bald, but in reality he had thick gray hair.

"We often sit here, Mai and I. We talk about work issues. I've come to rely on her greatly these past few months. She has keen insight. And we talk about her reading too, of course. See …" He pointed towards a corner of the library. "Those are your books."

Looking at where he was pointing, I recognized the cover of one of my books.

"Where does Mai work?" I asked.

"She works as general manager for a group of my companies. She's a graduate of economics, from the United States. I never expected her to grasp so many techniques required to be successful in business so well and so soon. I quickly realized how good she can be, strategically. I soon moved her from running just one small company to a group of them. She's doing very well."

"With your guidance?"

Khalid smiled. "Increasingly less so."

His attitude was refreshing. Here is a theme for the novel developing, I thought. Yes, Khalid the character, not a traditional businessman, but progressive, advancing certain causes perhaps.

The door opened and the Filipina girl came in, carrying a tray with two glasses of lemon juice. She gently placed the tray on the table before leaving without a word.

The room was calm.

"So, how are you going to record our conversations? A tape recorder?" Khalid asked.

"No, actually I prefer pen and paper. You will speak and I will write. The details I will write down, of course, but some of the information I will naturally take in – characteristics about you, for example, and how I will portray your character positively in the novel."

"That should be easy, shouldn't it? Here I am in front of you."

I smiled and said, "You're a real person right now. I will need you to be Khalid Khalifa, the novel's protagonist. We'll have to pass through the 'magic gate' to leave reality behind and enter the land of art and writing."

"OK. So, where shall we start?"

"As you wish."

"Right. I'll talk and you can stop me at any time to ask for information."

Khalid began to speak, though more to himself than to me. "I came from a middle-class family. I was the third child. There are four of us: two boys and two girls. My father, Salem, may God bless his soul, was a simple civil servant in the Ministry of Health, and my mother, may God bless her too, spent all her life at home, working for her family."

"What was your house like? How many bedrooms did it have?" I asked.

"Three. The first was for my dad and mom, the second for us boys, and the third for the girls."

"What else do you remember about your house?"

He smiled. "Ah, that's easy. The yard and the *sidra* tree. We gathered in the yard every evening to chat and later to watch a little black-and-white TV."

"Was it big, the yard?"

"During my childhood I thought it was! But just before they demolished the house in the mid-seventies, I visited it for the last time, and it looked so small! The rooms too, of course. And I wondered how we ever used to live in them. How on earth was the house ever big enough for six of us?!" He paused for a few seconds, then asked me, "Will all our meetings be like this? You're doing more asking than I'm speaking."

"I'd like to know everything about you."

"But that would mean I don't get to talk about the things on my mind."

"Why not?"

"I'll answer your questions and forget what I planned to say."

Don't cede control here, I said to myself. He's talking to you now like he does to his employees.

After a moment of silence, Khalid continued. "I studied at the primary school at Alsabah, the middle school at Alsaddeq, and I completed high school – "

"Sorry," I cut in. "You skipped a number of stages." He looked at me quizzically. "In one sentence you jumped over twelve years!"

"What do you want me to say?"

"I want to know the details of your life, your family, your social situation, and your relationship with your mother, father, and your brother and sisters. I want to know about your relationships with your friends, girls, about your adolescence."

There was an awkward silence and I began to have more second thoughts about the wisdom of taking on this assignment.

Khalid sighed. "Mai put me in this dilemma, you know," he said.

"Constructing a novel is never an easy task."

"Unfortunately."

He paused again. I didn't know what to do. It was already half past nine.

Then I had a sudden idea – incense.

Khalid looked up.

"May we perhaps have some incense?" I asked.

He smiled and got up, opened the door, and called a name. After a few seconds, the Filipina girl rushed in.

"Bring the incense burner," he said, then came back over and sat down.

"If you don't want to talk anymore today, then how about we finish for tonight?" I suggested. "If you want to cancel the contract even, I don't mind. I haven't touched the down payment."

He smiled. "Oh, please forget the payment, it's fine. You know, I was actually expecting a moment like this."

Mai came in, carrying the incense burner. "Good evening," she said, walking over to her father. "You look a little anxious."

She was wearing a gray tracksuit, her hair in a ponytail.

"A dilemma," Khalid said simply.

He took the words out of my mouth. Mai looked at me, but I couldn't think what I ought to say.

"What happened?" Mai asked.

"Mr. Alrefai wants to know all the details of my life … But … well, this is very difficult."

She turned, looking at me as if for confirmation.

"True, I need to know all kinds of details in order to write the novel," I said. "I told your father that I'm ready to withdraw from the contract and give back the down payment if he wishes – I don't want to upset anyone."

"I'm not upset or annoyed, no," Khalid cut in. "It's just that, well, the situation is difficult. I have to share details of my life, but it's not easy."

Khalid checked his watch. "Excuse me for a few minutes, would you? I must make a phone call. Time zone differences, you see."

"Of course," I said.

"Perhaps Mr. Alrefai and I could sit together a while," Mai suggested. "I don't often get to meet many writers I admire."

Khalid rose. "Why not? I'll leave you two for a few minutes. I'll be back as soon as I can."

"I'm sorry your father is upset," I said.

"I don't think he is, really. This is your first meeting and it's not so unusual to come up against difficulties." She looked in my eyes as if revealing a secret. "My father … He suffers from high blood pressure and has heart palpitations. The doctor advised him to avoid tension."

"I see. I'm sorry, I don't want to cause any problems."

"On the contrary. He's going through a hard time and perhaps his engagement with the novel will help him get over it." I wondered what hard time her father was going through. Just his health or something between him and his wife?

"For months we've been talking about doing this novel. I convinced him to enjoy this experiment. He'll tell you his life story and you'll write it. I don't want the novel to be, you know, 'traditional' so that people can ignore it. I like your writing and I think that my father's life story is interesting, so it will make for a novel with a difference."

I couldn't deny that I liked what she said. "Writing a biographical novel is rather different from writing a normal novel, though," I said. "I have to know everything about your father. He's the protagonist. I can't simply invent him."

"I understand."

"And writing a novel about a real person who is well known in the community requires a certain caution. People will read it and compare what they know with what the novel says. This requires a meticulous approach and careful writing."

"Would you prefer it if I sit in with you?"

"That's up to your father. Few people have the courage to strip themselves bare in front of their children, though." I read a look of surprise in her eyes and added, "Your presence might stop him from talking about some private things."

She shook her head. "I don't think my father hides any of his life's secrets from me."

"I don't know. Every human being has secrets not seen by

anyone, secret moments of weakness, of cruelty, lies, aggression, and possibly humiliation." I noticed a look of slight annoyance on her face. "Sorry, I don't specifically mean your father, of course. I'm speaking generally here. But he won't be different in some of these aspects at least. It's human nature."

We paused and I thought of my daughter Farah and how similar she was to Mai. Mai was as concerned about her father as Farah was about me. I smiled, picturing Mai on a computer screen, checking up on Khalid during the day. Perhaps I could include such a scene to show their close relationship. He certainly placed great trust in her. And the way his face softened when she was in the room was clear for anyone to see. I was the same with Farah, I thought. I had a special relationship with her. Perhaps it was because she was the elder daughter. For fifteen years, we had enjoyed a special relationship before it changed a little when Fadia was born.

With Farah, I shared her childhood with her, relishing being a father in his twenties. I got to relive childhood in a way, with all the playing, the games, and the teaching and learning from each other.

As she got older, I would drive her to school every morning. We would listen to the radio and sing together on the way. And on the way home, we would talk about our day and she would tell me about the things that were on her mind. I was proud of her little achievements and later her academic success, especially as she surpassed all my friends' children all through school.

Farah came along when I was just twenty-six years old. I was forty-one when Fadia was born. I was thrilled. Of course I was. During her childhood, though, I began to understand the importance of my age difference. I didn't play with Fadia as much as I had with Farah, and I couldn't run around with her in the same way as I had when I was younger. I relied much more on Shoroq to share the load.

I was trying my best to spend quality time with Fadia. But my life had changed since my first go at fatherhood, with my reading and writing. Even my friendships had changed.

When Farah was awarded her Bachelor's degree from Kuwait University and then went to the United States to do her Master's, the separation was a wrench, a great emptiness in my life where she used to be every day. Phone calls with video had helped, of course, but it was still not easy to be separated by continents from your firstborn.

"How were your studies in America?" I asked Mai.

"Good overall. Sometimes it was hard being away, of course. But I learned so much and made some good friends," she replied. Suddenly she added, "Please be patient with him, won't you? My father, he *is* a kind man." Daughters and their fathers, I thought.

I saw a glimpse of expectation in her eyes. "Of course. I'll let your father talk as he wishes and I'll try to write the novel as best I can," I said.

"Dinner is ready." Khalid had come in. He looked at Mai and then turned to me, "You haven't been harassing Mai, I hope?"

I smiled. "It seems that I upset everyone here."

He smiled. "Come," he beckoned and gently helped me up.

"I don't usually eat dinner," I said, a little embarrassed. Everything in his house was new to me. I wondered how friendship was born between human beings. My mother always said, "Make as many friends as you can and avoid having even a single enemy."

"Well, just don't eat too much, then," Khalid joked, still holding my hand. "Let me tell you something. If I hadn't felt comfortable with you from our first meeting, I wouldn't have invited you to my house, so please join us."

"Thank you."

"I believe there is chemistry between human beings," Khalid said as we walked out. "Some souls are attracted to each other and others are repelled. My heart accepts some people from the first meeting, and rejects others, who I prefer to stay away from."

"Thank God your heart accepts me," I said with a smile.

I was struck again by how everything around me was different for me: the design of the place, the lighting, the alcoves, the colors of the walls, the marble, the carpets. And my presence in a house with people I didn't know. Nothing felt familiar. But it would help me recreate the world of the character in the novel.

We went into a small dining area connected to a kitchenette, with high chairs.

"Mai and I prefer to eat a light meal, as you can see." The way Khalid and his daughter talked about each other suggested they lived alone in the house.

"I prepared it myself," Mai said. "It's just a simple meal."

I took a look at the dining table and smiled at her. I saw cucumbers, tomatoes, a dish of boiled vegetables, many types of cheeses, olives, an arugula salad platter, hummus, a dish of kubba, a basket of bread, and a basket of fruit.

"This is quite a full dinner!" I joked to Mai. "It looks like Mr. Khalifa loves his food!"

I had a strange feeling. It was the first time I had sat down to eat with Khalid and his daughter. He treated me as if I were a family friend. Usually it was difficult for Kuwaitis to let a stranger into their homes and have him sit with their wives or daughters. Men had friendships in their own separate world, away from the family atmosphere and from women. Friends met in the *diwaniya*, part of the house but segregated from the women's areas.

Such gatherings usually took place every night for decades so the men became like brothers, without ever seeing the face of the other man's wife or ever visiting him inside his home.

After our two meetings in his office, I had assumed we would talk in his office again, away from the family, yet Khalid had arranged this meeting at his home with his daughter. It was very much an asset in helping me paint the character of the man.

"Please, feel free and eat whatever you wish," Khalid said.

I was still feeling a little hesitant so I served myself just a small piece of brown bread, some tomatoes, olives, and cucumber.

"Taleb prefers to be the listener all the time," Khalid said to Mai.

"Ah, well, silence is the writer's friend," I said.

Mai was smiling. "Mr. Alrefai isn't speaking much because he's thinking about the novel perhaps."

I smiled too. "You'll have to excuse me. I don't really know how I'm going to write the novel yet, and whether it would be right for me to mention certain details."

"Which details?" Khalid asked.

"Details of your house, your thoughts, and your relationship with Mai."

"You will write about me without any family involvement," he said, looking straight at me. "My wife, Awatef, doesn't like the idea of this novel."

So there was a problem in the background, I thought.

"I don't know why she's annoyed about it," he continued. "I tried to discuss the idea with her but she refused and rejected the idea of a novel about my life." He sounded a little breathless as he spoke. "Awatef has her own ideas. Things I don't really understand. Anyway, let's get back to my story. As I told you, I lived in a middle-class family …"

"What about your family now?" I asked, pausing from dipping my bread into the oil around the olives. The olives were as exquisite as I'd ever tasted.

"I have two girls and one boy. Mai is twenty-nine years old, Walid is twenty-five – he's studying in America now – and Mona is twenty-one. As I said, my father worked in the Ministry of Health. He had two brothers and he was the poorest among them. My Uncle Abdul-Aziz was in business and my Uncle Fahad was a senior official in the Ministry of Works. When I asked my father why we were poor, he only said, 'Thank God for everything we have.' God bless his soul. He lived and died contented, always saying, 'God gives every man his share in life.'"

Khalid paused for a few seconds to catch his breath before continuing. "Even though my father was a simple man, he was in love with reading – something he planted in me."

He turned to Mai and asked her for some orange juice.

"Let me write down some of this," I said, pleased that he was starting to talk more freely.

"Yes, of course." He gave me a minute before he continued. "In the early seventies, we moved to live in a new area after my father got a free house given by the government to Kuwaiti citizens with lower incomes. The first thing that drew my attention to the differences in social levels was my Uncle Fahad. His house was so big! He had more than just cars – he had drivers, servants, and people to farm his land. In the summer months, he traveled with his family to Lebanon or Cairo and later to London. He had his own spacious *diwaniya* in his house, where he would meet his friends every night. I remember when I went with my father to visit his *diwaniya* and I sensed how rich he was and how a government position could bring power and confidence to a person. I was upset at my father's weakness and our poverty." He paused for a few seconds. "What hurt me most were both the patronizing looks and the contempt that my Uncle Fahad and his sons treated us with. I can't describe how that irritated me."

Both Mai and I had stopped eating, caught up in Khalid's memories.

"There's an incident imprinted on my memory. One night, my father took me to visit Uncle Fahad's *diwaniya*, and there I discovered that the occasion was to see my uncle off before he traveled to Lebanon. We sat in the *diwaniya* silently as if we were not relatives. When my father shook Uncle Fahad's hand and said goodbye to his brother, my uncle said loudly, so everybody in the *diwaniya* could hear, 'Next year, I'll take you with us to Lebanon.' Poor Dad. He nodded and simply replied weakly, 'Thanks, may God give you more.'

"When we got back to the car, for some reason tears came to my eyes. I cried bitterly, and when my father asked why, I said, 'Because of my uncle!' And I begged him, 'Please, Dad, don't go abroad with him next year.'"

Khalid's story seemed to be new to Mai and I could clearly see the pained look on her face.

"My uncle's wife, though, was a kind woman. She would come by from time to time to visit with my mother. She brought many gifts, and before she would leave she used to give my mother some money as charity. I'll always remember my mother's face when she put out her hand and said in a broken voice, 'Thanks ... thanks.'"

Khalid stopped and looked at Mai. "This wasn't a good idea of yours. I'll suffer a lot. I feel a tightness in my chest when I recall those memories."

A horrified look crossed Mai's face. "Sorry," she said. "Please, drink a little juice."

After a moment, Khalid continued. "Something important I have to mention to you. I was on the honors list at school, the same school where my uncle's sons were so lazy. I realized that, although my uncle was rich and could simply take his sons to Lebanon or anywhere, he couldn't make them better than me academically. From then on, I began to read and memorize everything I read. I loved reading novels, poetry, and books on philosophy. Years later, I had collected hundreds of books. I finished high school with honors, which meant I could choose any college at Kuwait University. In 1971, I joined the College of Commerce and Economics and Political Science."

"Why did you choose that college?"

"Because I wanted to learn something with which I could stand up to my Uncle Fahad."

"Did you do so?"

"Yes, but in another way."

He looked at his watch, and at the same moment, I felt my back pain.

"Since you're reluctant to eat much, perhaps we should go back to continue our conversation in the office."

"If you don't mind, could we continue another time? I have to sort through all this information."

"Of course."

I took my leave of Mai as we stood up. I walked out with Khalid, passing through the library and the dining room. He walked with me silently to the front door, where we bade each other good night.

I walked to my car, thinking about this man who would take the lead role in the novel that I intended to write.

Chapter 5

Thursday, April 19, 2007

"Please don't be late," I said to Shoroq. "I promised Mr. Khalifa we would be there by eleven. I want to be sure we arrive on time."

I knew Shoroq would only get anxious if I hung around watching her while she dressed and put on her makeup, so I left. "I'll wait for you down in my office."

I went downstairs and through the hall to my office. We were supposed to leave the house to reach Khalid's beach house at half past ten but, as usual, Shoroq would make us late. Ever since we married, we had tended to argue before leaving the house. I always felt that I had to seize each moment. I tried to make the best of every minute of my life. Shoroq, however, was always happily relaxed. It bothered me to be late for any appointment – even five minutes – and although she knew this, she never moved at anything but her own pace. Whenever we attended an event, I warned her early about the time we needed to leave, and I repeated it, several times sometimes. But every time she was late. I would wait and have to call her until I almost lost my temper and started screaming! This upset her, of course, spoiling the evening before it had even started.

I wished we could leave on time, even once. This time especially. This was the first time Khalid had invited us over together to meet his family. I still didn't know how I was going to write the novel, but clearly it had to be based partly on the real man and partly on my imagination. I had to deal with him as a reality. I had to be honest about the real him and his life. I would portray Khalid as I saw him and heard him, of course, but the real difficulty would lie in the transfer of fact into art. The fact that Khalid and his wife were both millionaires made him a good subject, and I could use it as an opportunity to write about Kuwaiti society. Some people believed that wealth brought happiness but I didn't. In this experiment I would learn about a real case and write it up. I had previously written about foreigners in Kuwait, so Khalid's family offered a new angle.

The fact that the whole family was rich meant it would be hard to introduce any contrast. Then I remembered that Khalid's family hadn't been rich in his youth, so the contrast would lie there.

"Shoroq!" I yelled. "We're late!"

"I'm coming! Just a few more minutes!"

A few more minutes ... I was convinced that one of the things that could lead to the failure of any marriage was incompatibility in certain key things, like where to live, how to bring up your children ... and punctuality!

A minute later, I heard Shoroq bustling and I looked up.

"Sorry. Fadia made me late," Shoroq said, coming into my office.

I looked at my watch.

"We're not late," she said.

"Come on then, let's go." I rose and headed back out to the hall, where Fadia was waiting.

Shoroq busied herself, putting on Fadia's shoes and checking their hair. Outside, I helped Shoroq fasten Fadia into her seat in the car, smoothing out the folds in her clothes for her.

As we left the house, Shoroq suggested we ought to take something for Khalid with us, so we stopped by a bakery to buy a basket of pastries and another of sweets.

We set off again along King Fahad Road towards Khalid's beach house.

***

Two days earlier, my friend Suleiman and his wife Samar had come to visit us. Samar loved Fadia and brought a new toy for her whenever she came over. Or else she took Fadia to McDonald's, although Shoroq didn't usually allow that.

"I was a bit tough on her today," Suleiman had whispered to me. "Let's go down to your office."

"She's gone mad and is driving me crazy!" he said when we'd sat down. "This is her third IVF failure in seven months. She's tired, and so am I. After the last IVF, the doctor told her there was a very good chance of pregnancy. But this morning she woke up with stomach pain. And later on, she started bleeding," he said bitterly.

I felt desperately sorry for him. "I'm sorry to hear that."

"Our life has turned into hell!" he said. "Day and night, we talk about nothing but pregnancy! I know she's in her forties now and I know her chances of pregnancy are obviously declining, and all of her friends have three or four children. The sight of any child gets her thinking about a child of her own. And it simply hurts her."

I could only nod.

"Trying for an IVF baby is a tedious process. It's long and painful, what with Samar's injections to stimulate the development of her eggs, the doctor retrieving the eggs, mixing them with the sperm cells for forty-eight hours, and then the fertilization. Then, if that works, Samar is called to the hospital again to transfer the embryo into her uterus. More endless injections to ensure the transferred embryo is successfully implanted. And waiting and waiting …

"And I really detest that moment the doctor asks me to give a sample of semen – you know, for insemination. The nurse gives me the sample cup and I go into a private room and into the bathroom. I take off my clothes and stand in front of the mirror, ashamed of myself. I'm trying to imagine an image – any image – and then … you know. It's a miserable moment. I ejaculate into the cup, get dressed, and leave. At that moment, I hate everything around me and feel disgusted with myself!"

I didn't speak. I really didn't know how to console him.

"I'll be fifty soon," Suleiman continued. "So I suggested we adopt a child. Since we live in a society that doesn't really approve of that, I told Samar we could travel somewhere and then bring the child back and tell everyone it's our baby." He sighed deeply. "It's all we talk about every day."

I wished I could help him.

"Do you know what hurts most in the artificial insemination process?" he said.

"No."

"When we started the process, we began a new journey – a small crumb of hope for Samar. But through all the waiting, she soon began asking me every minute, 'What do you think? Will I get pregnant this time?'

"'God willing,' I keep replying – over and over. Then the waiting turns into a monster, and every casual incident becomes some metaphysical sign about pregnancy." He's blaming things on Samar's insistence on a baby, I thought to myself.

I nodded and reminded Suleiman that Samar was his sweetheart and that she was a wonderful woman who had endured so much. She had exposed herself to gossip by agreeing to live with him for years before their marriage, flouting social norms. Moreover, she was a caring woman who had helped Suleiman get over the death of his mother.

Suleiman listened with a look in his eyes that said, "I know, I know."

Children. They gave us heartache even before they were born.

***

Traffic was moving quite quickly on King Fahad Road. I pressed my foot down on the gas pedal a little and cruised along.

"You're sure they won't be annoyed by us visiting them?" Shoroq asked.

"Yes, I'm sure."

"Even me and Fadia?"

"Khalid told me his daughter Mai and her son are waiting for your visit."

Shoroq was silent for a few seconds. Then she said, "Samar is thinking of adopting, you know."

"Yes. What did you say to her?"

"To think it over carefully and contact specialized hospitals and centers outside Kuwait. She's thinking of using a donated egg. In Europe, there are special egg-donation centers. Suleiman must fertilize the egg, of course. Do you think he'll agree?"

"Why not? She'll get pregnant and finally they'll have a baby. But even if not, many couples have lived without children."

"But are they fulfilled?" Shoroq said.

I recognized Shoroq's feelings on the subject. I smiled at her. I couldn't argue with her. Where would our lives be without Farah and Fadia?

The beach houses in the Julai'a area were on the left-hand side of the road. I had been given the intersection number and

Khalid had promised that the driver of his BMW jeep would be waiting for me at the side of the road.

I saw a jeep that matched the description and brought the car to a halt. "You're Mr. Khalifa's driver?" I asked.

"Yes, Mr. Alrefai? Please follow me." I was going to see a new side of Khalid's life. The first and second times, I had met him in his office, the third at his home. But now we were going to meet in his beach house, in a family setting.

The driver pulled into the driveway.

"Welcome, welcome," Khalid, dressed in sports clothes and shoes, said the moment I opened the car door. Perhaps he had been waiting for us.

In the driveway stood a Mercedes, a Lexus, a GMC, and a Chevrolet Caprice. I noticed a jet ski too.

"Sorry we're late," I said.

"It's fine, you're not late."

I reached into the car and took out the baskets of pastries and sweets while Khalid greeted Shoroq.

"Welcome, Shoroq. I'm delighted to meet you." He shook hands with her and bent over to kiss Fadia. "I'll call Adel over to play with you," he told her.

Fadia looked overjoyed.

"Fadia's a carbon copy of her mother!" he said, and Shoroq smiled.

"Come in, please. We're waiting for you."

Mai walked over, smiling and holding her son's hand.

"This is Mai and this is Adel," Khalid said.

"This is my wife Shoroq and this is Fadia," I told Mai.

Shoroq shook hands with Mai and kissed Adel as Mai kissed Fadia. We went into a spacious hall with a tiled floor and several chairs. On the right stood a dining table. I went over to it to put down the baskets.

"Thank you," said Mai.

"This is my mother," said Khalid, pointing toward a woman who looked to be in her late seventies. Her face suggested warmth and contentment.

Shoroq went over to her and said, "Hello. How are you?"

"I'm fine, thanks be to God," she answered in a soft voice. She looks like my mother, I thought. But maybe all aging mothers had something in common. I noticed that she smelled of incense and perfumed wood.

"Would you like to sit and rest for a little bit or we shall start our meeting?" Khalid asked me. I look at Shoroq, but before she could respond, he added, "Perhaps it would better to start our meeting and have Shoroq stay with my mother and Mai."

"As you wish."

"We'll leave Shoroq and Fadia with you," Khalid said to Mai. "See you at lunch later."

He was treating us as if we were longtime friends.

Fadia went over to sit near Adel, who was almost her age.

"Please have a seat," Mai said to Shoroq.

Khalid turned and left the room, and I followed him down a corridor separating two beach houses built in the Greek rustic style: white walls with blue aluminum windows. The frontage on the sea stretched almost fifty meters. I estimated the floor area of the beach house at around 1,000 square meters.

The sea was distant, like a still blue-and-white mirror. A pleasant breeze was blowing.

This is the protagonist of my novel, actually walking in front of me, I reflected. I thought how I might include the beach house in the novel. Could a novel really encapsulate someone's life?

"This is my special beach house," Khalid said, stopping at the threshold. "I often come here, away from any distractions, with no one except the sea, a book, and some movies."

We entered a large room, bathed in light, facing directly out to sea, and connected to another room. I recalled what Suleiman had said about the rumor that he was separated from his wife.

"I've not seen Madam," I said to Khalid carefully.

He looked at me curiously as if he knew what lay behind my question. "She won't be coming today," he said.

His answer was hiding something, but I told myself not to press the subject. He had the right not to tell me about his issues with his wife.

We sat on a comfortable sofa facing the sea.

"Do you have any shares in the stock market?" Khalid asked.

"No, I don't."

"You didn't read the newspapers today? Yesterday was an unusual day for the Kuwait Stock Exchange. The volume of trade was more than 1.8 billion Kuwaiti dinars. That's more than 6.5 billion U.S. dollars. Can you imagine that?"

I wanted to tell him that I had never entered the stock exchange building. I barely even looked at it if I ever went past it.

"This is probably a singular situation, though markets have a habit of stabilizing. In fact, I'm actually wondering whether a financial disaster is on its way."

The tide was slowly receding as our meeting progressed. I looked at Khalid and I didn't know what to say.

"Do you know where the paradox lies?" he asked.

"Where?"

"The stock exchange turns over billions in a day while Kuwaiti citizens have to wait twenty years to get a government house."

I was surprised at this comment. Why was he thinking about this? Maybe it was because his father hadn't been wealthy and one day had received a government house.

I liked the sea view. Sitting here was conducive to relaxation and meditation. Music, books, and the sea ... what a lovely place! With a pretty woman, it would be wonderful, I mused.

"Have you started to put together a plan for the novel?" Khalid asked me.

"Are you still sure about using your real name?" I asked.

"Of course, my real name is the novel. I want people to know how I built myself."

At least he knows what he wants, I thought.

Suleiman had told me that Kuwaitis knew that Abdul Razzaq Al-Abdullatif, Khalid's father-in-law, was the man who had made him.

"If I use your real name, it will cast a shadow on your wife, your son, and your daughters," I said.

"Please, keep the focus away from my wife," he said. "As I told you, she's against me having this novel written. I'll tell you something I didn't intend to ..." He stopped and looked out to sea for a few seconds.

"The moment we signed the contract, I felt that this would give me a good opportunity to say a lot of things that have been weighing on me and to document some of my experiences." He continued, breathing more rapidly, "Perhaps the novel will bother some people, but that's stuff from thirty years ago. As for me, I suffer daily."

Suddenly he fell silent. Who are these *some people* he mentioned? I wondered.

Khalid looked at me in a way I didn't understand. "What would you like to drink?" he asked.

"Oh, I'll have whatever you're drinking."

"I'll have fresh orange juice."

"Fine, just as you're having, thank you."

He got up and went to the refrigerator. I noticed a hardback copy of *Silent House* by the Turkish novelist Orhan Pamuk sitting on the table in front of me. It felt like the sea and the light were sitting in with us and I recalled an old dream in which I had a small house on a riverbank.

"There you are." Khalid put the glass of juice in front of me. "You asked me about my wife. I don't know how you're going to write about that. Awatef called me yesterday and assured me again that she objected to the book." He paused for a few seconds before continuing. "She seems to have a number of fears about it, though I don't know why. So, you won't have any communication with her. You'll just write the novel and I'll check it when it's finished."

His decree annoyed me but I didn't speak.

"Being with Awatef has been the most important thing in my life, I have to admit that. My world was formed in her hands. The good things I have had all came with her and what I suffer now is because of her." As if consoling himself, he added, "Life gives on one side and takes from the other. When I started at Kuwait University, I asked my Uncle Fahad to help by arranging work for me in the evenings. He found me work in the emergency section of the electricity and water department. I received complaints of incidents from the public over the telephone, took down their addresses and told the engineers and technicians where to go. I was studying at the university in the morning and working at night. I was cut off from the world of leisure and girls. I was determined to set myself up and buy a car. My friend Nasser would drive me to the university in the morning and I would take a taxi to go back home."

I was starting to get used to his heavy breathing. And I felt that some connection was also starting to form between us.

"Nasser Alnasser is my lifelong friend," he said.

"The former minister?"

"Yes."

"Our friendship began in middle school. Nasser was, and still is, closer to me than my brother. We studied together, travelled together and held secrets together. For years, I used to go to his *diwaniya*, but when he moved to his new home, he set up a special corner for us to talk, and since then, this corner has become our favorite place. We meet weekly. When I arrive, I find him waiting for me under soft lighting and listening to music. We meet at nine and go on until eleven-thirty or twelve."

An image of the former minister took shape in my mind.

"Please, I don't want any mention of Nasser in the novel."

I was confused. What would Khalid let me write about?

"You mentioned your friendship and that he's your best friend, so why can't I write about that?"

"I'll tell you many things for clarification, but you're not to write everything. Choose only what doesn't affect the reputation of my family."

I nodded. I had thought I was working out how to structure the novel, but elements I would expect to include were now being denied me. He looked at me.

"Go ahead, say whatever you want," I said. "Speak about everything and I will write about only the important events."

"No. You will only write what I allow."

His blunt manner bothered me, but I knew that he who pays the piper calls the tune.

"Every morning, Nasser took me to the university. I would go back home for lunch, and in the evening my father would drive me to the electricity emergency center. I came back home in a ministry car with foreign workers.

"My brother Saleh bought a car when he graduated from the police academy. My father helped him pay the deposit. But I didn't want to put more of a burden on my father – he was only a low-level civil servant and his salary barely covered our expenses at home."

Suddenly he stopped and our eyes met. "I wonder what's going on! I'm telling you all the secrets of my life, although this is difficult for me," he continued.

"I know," I said. He kept looking at me. "Both of us are at the same scene but each in his own corner."

"You and Mai have pushed me here."

I smiled. "I'm not responsible for anything. I want this to be easy on you, for you to talk about what you want to, rather than me asking you a lot of questions. I don't want you to feel like I'm interrogating you. This isn't an article, after all." Again I noticed how pleasant the sea looked.

"Awatef came my way during college. I was in my second year. She is two years older than me. We were taking the same economics class. Our relationship began the day she asked for my notes, the day I saw her for the first time. She told me she'd missed a couple of classes the previous week and had noticed I took a lot of notes.

"'Sorry, no,' I told her. She stood defiantly in front of me and asked why not.

"'I don't like to give my work to anybody,' I told her.

"I was in a hurry, so I left her and walked on. But something was needling me when I saw her in the next lecture. I could see she was annoyed from her eyes and her face, but the most important thing was that I now paid attention to her presence. Later on, I found out she was the daughter of the billionaire businessman Abdul Razzaq Al-Abdullatif.

"Awatef might not be an outstanding beauty, but what attracted me to her the most was the pride she showed. And there was something about her that showed she came from a well-off and prestigious house. I have to confess that my view of her changed the moment I realized she was Al-Abdullatif's daughter."

It was strange what was going on between us. It was a new experience for me as a writer. A man I didn't know had become a part of my life, my day, my writing. Without prior warning, he had dragged me into his world, taking me to his office and his home and introducing me to his family. And now he was telling me the details of his life, tossing his memories out to me, and I found myself becoming wrapped up in his life. He was the omniscient narrator and I was the listener. Rather a reversal of roles for me.

Khalid was telling me the details of his life, but how was I going to lay out his memories and life in a novel that couldn't include his family or his best friend?

After my last meeting with Khalid, I had opened a new file on my PC. I had hesitated for a moment because I didn't know what to name it. Finally, I simply wrote "Khalid Khalifa" and then proceeded to write down all the information I had recorded.

"When I decided to introduce myself to Awatef," Khalid continued, "I wasn't thinking about getting married. I liked the idea that she could be my girlfriend and I liked even more the idea that I could belong to her world. I was proud to walk beside her! Awatef Al-Abdullatif, the billionaire's daughter – oh my God!" He was silent for a while.

"That is how my life changed!" he finally said, as if talking to himself.

Khalid took a deep breath and continued, "Anyway, Kuwait University in the seventies was completely different than it is now. It was part of one of the most beautiful and most important periods of development and openness. Alwasat, the democratic student movement, was in control in the National Union of Students. Male and female students had open and respectful relationships and went to concerts together. Kuwaiti society at that time was detached from religious influences. It was one of the most wonderful periods of prosperity – socially, economically, artistically, and athletically, both locally and internationally. Kuwait at that time was a beacon of light in the Gulf. No other country could compete with it."

Khalid wheezed as he struggled to finish his last sentence: "I feel sad when I look at Kuwait's situation today. Everything has changed."

"Change is life," I said.

"I think our society's changes are not for the better. The people of Kuwait pine for the days of the seventies."

"Some are happy."

"The religious and tribally oriented, yes."

"Tomorrow is the most beautiful of days," I said. Khalid looked at me. "Hope hides in the womb of the future," I added.

"Drink your juice," he said, picking up his own.

The sea looked still.

"Suddenly, my life path changed. Before I met Awatef, I was worried about having pocket money and buying a car in installments, but the day I decided to be her friend my thinking changed. She became the focus of my life. It was the first time the needs and wants of any girl had found a place in my thinking. Her very inaccessibility made her a dream, so I had to remove any obstacle that might stand between her and me. I copied my entire notebook in beautiful handwriting and I waited for my chance.

"I stopped her at the end of one of the lectures and held out the notebook, looking into her eyes. 'Please,' I said.

"'What's this?'

"'The course notes.'

"'Thank you, I don't need them,' she told me.

"My hand remained outstretched, but she drew back, disdainful. Walking away was her way of striking back at me. I followed her and stopped her.

"'I've copied all the lectures,' I said.

"'I told you, I don't need them.' She looked straight into my eyes and said, 'You don't like to give your work to anybody.'

"'I'm sorry,' I said and offered the notebook to her again. 'Please accept it. It's for you.'

"You know …" he smiled at me, "my heart really pounded when she reached out and took the notebook."

It was a touching little anecdote but could I use it? Khalid had said he didn't want me to write anything about his wife, and the lawyer had advised me to be careful.

Suddenly the door opened and I looked up to see Fadia running toward me.

"Papa!"

Adel followed her and ran to his grandfather's lap. Mai and Shoroq stood near the door. "When would you like to eat?" Mai asked her father.

"As you like," Khalid said, and invited Shoroq to come in.

"We need another half an hour, and then we'll come to you," he told Mai.

"Have you thought of a title for the novel?" Mai asked me.

"The title is one of the hardest things in the whole novel!" I said.

"My father and I thought of a number of titles." She took a piece of paper out of her pocket and began to read. "*Khalid Khalifa: A Biography* or *A Success Story*, or *The Life of Man*. I like the title *Another Life*."

She folded up the paper and looked at me, waiting for a response. I hesitated before saying courteously, "Yes, good titles."

I looked at Shoroq's face, trying to work out how contented she was, but I couldn't.

"The sea view from here is very nice," she said to Khalid.

"It is. I like it especially at sunrise."

He got up to open the window. A cool breeze blew in. The shoreline was still receding with the tide.

"When are we going to swim in the sea?" Fadia asked me.

"In the summer," I said.

Adel stepped up to stand by Fadia.

"They've become friends," said Mai.

"He's going to come home with me," Fadia announced.

Shoroq interceded: "We've made plans. We will go out, Mai and I, early in the week to have coffee."

"What about me and Adel?" Fadia asked nervously.

Her mother smiled. "You too."

Khalid laughed and told Mai, "We'll come to you in half an hour."

"Lunch will be ready by then."

Everyone left.

Khalid returned to his narration: "In the seventies, there was no segregation between boys and girls. After a few sessions in the library and cafeteria with Awatef, she gave me the telephone number of her room and her car phone. I still hadn't bought a car. We became friends and we would spend parts of the day together, in the auditorium, the library, the cafeteria, and the garden. She started to come to university concerts with me, and every night we stayed awake until dawn talking on the phone. Perhaps it doesn't sound so exciting, but to us it was. Awatef was always a traditional girl so our courtship was perhaps traditional, looking back. I'll never forget her eyes, so dark, so intense. And the way she looked at me, as if I was the only other person on the planet. She treated me like her prince. I never felt so special in all my life.

"I remember what my friend Nasser told me: that all my friends at university envied me. That they called me 'Lucky Khalid,' and said I'd snatched the treasure, and people had started to speak of us as 'Handsome and the Treasure'!"

Khalid paused.

I realized I would have to meet this Nasser, as well as Awatef.

The sea was still observing us, I noticed, whenever I glanced at it.

"Because she was Abdullatif's daughter, everyone was hovering around," Khalid continued.

For a second I thought of asking him whether Nasser was one of them. But I didn't and even if Nasser had been there I would have had to write him in as someone else.

"There are things I'll never forget. One night, when we were talking on the telephone, she asked me, 'What do I mean to you?'

"'You are everything in my life,' I replied without thinking. Nearly a year had passed in our relationship then."

He looked at me, as if remembering something important. "What I'm saying is for you, not for publication. I don't want people to know the secrets of my relationship with my wife, and I don't want her to think I'm writing this novel to expose our secrets. Please, don't forget that we live in Kuwait. I'm trusting you with this information and I will not allow anyone else to know about it."

I understood his point of view, but it certainly complicated the process of writing an interesting novel.

"Write the novel without Awatef in it," Khalid continued.

I thought of responding that I wished I could, but that it wouldn't be possible. In the end I put it as a question: "It's a biographical novel. How can I take out your life and family?"

"I don't want any problems with Awatef and her family. I will leave this for you to solve."

The pleasant sea breeze blew in through the window.

Khalid said, "The day I told Awatef that she was everything in my life, she asked me how long she would stay everything in my life."

He picked up his juice and looked out to sea.

"Despite all that stands between us, still she is ..."

He left his phrase hanging and I noticed that a chill had crept into the room. I wished he would say what was going on between them.

"Awatef told her mother she'd met someone at university and that she wanted to marry him. After a while, she told me her dad's secretary would call me to meet him.

"The first time I went to meet Abdul Razzaq Al-Abdullatif, he kept me waiting for about an hour. When I finally went into his office, he asked me directly my father's name. I replied, 'Salem Khalifa.'

"He asked me if Fahad Khalifa at the Ministry of Works was my uncle.

"I told him yes. Then he asked me about my job and I told him I was still a student at the university and I was also working at the department of electricity in the evening. He asked me about our house. I had to tell him it was a government house for people with limited incomes. I stuttered as I said it and I still remember his sharp look. 'In the Sulaibikhat area,' I added.

"I don't know how these memories come to me. I never imagined they would be lying around in my head. I never thought I would tell them to anyone."

Khalid settled back on the sofa and continued his story. "Before I went to meet her father, Awatef and I planned everything I should say, and I had repeated it hundreds of times. But when I entered his office, my plans fell apart. Although he was a quiet man, I felt something intimidating surrounded him, and that made me reluctant to talk. There was an intensity in his voice when he asked me, 'What is there between you and my daughter?'

"I was frightened to tell him the truth about our relationship, so I said, 'Fellowship and friendship at university.'

"He looked into my face, trying to gauge the sincerity of my response.

"'What do you know about me?' he asked with a penetrating look.

"'Everybody knows the Al-Abdullatif family, of course. You are well known for your generosity and good reputation.'

"'What else?'

"'I am sure you are perceptive and understand that I have a pure and respectable love for your good daughter.'

"He narrowed his eyes and in a quiet but scary voice said to me, 'You will end your relationship with my daughter and look for another girl.'

"I hesitated to ask him what he thought his daughter might want. He simply pointed to the door and told me the meeting was over. I just looked at him and said thank you."

"Lunch is ready!" Mai announced, standing near the door.

Khalid was silent.

"We're coming," Khalid told Mai after a moment.

"Grandmother is hungry!"

Khalid stood up and walked in front of me.

I wished our meeting had been longer so I could find out more. I noticed that Mai was looking at Khalid, surprised by his silence. Quietly, she asked me what had happened.

"Nothing," I said simply.

Khalid's mother received us kindly. "Welcome. Please, lunch is ready."

We made our way over to the dining table and sat down.

Mai seems to be divorced, I said to myself.

I looked at her son and wondered about his father. A sudden sadness washed over me. Whenever I saw a sad woman, I thought of my mother and the pain she suffered because of her divorce and having her sons taken away from her.

Chapter 6

Monday, April 30, 2007

My appointment with Khalid was at half past nine in the evening.

From the moment I signed the contract, I felt I had added a new anxiety to the pile of my other concerns. I used to write freely without anyone giving me orders. I told Shoroq I wanted to give up my position as manager in the Culture and Arts Department of the National Council.

"The office work is exhausting and takes up all my time. I dream of having a few quiet moments to myself. The administrative duties, the meetings and committees. I'm always on the run. I have no time for writing. I'm seriously thinking of going back to the Engineering Department. At least it's a quiet place there and my duties are light, so I can read and write as I want."

"Yes, I see. That would probably be a good idea."

I was amazed at her immediate approval.

"Don't be angry or anything when I say I've been waiting for you to decide this," she said. "You're always worried and tense. Any time we discuss a topic you quickly get worked up and begin to yell. Even with little Fadia you've become tough. And your ulcers are returning. Look in the mirror and you can see how much older you've become of late."

Farah had wept when she spoke to me that morning and asked if I was OK.

When I answered yes, she burst into tears.

"That's not true! Fadia told me you were sick and you were in the hospital for surgery."

"Fadia is a child."

"Fadia's not lying to me! She said you have a problem with your stomach."

"I'm fine. It was just a check-up, a one-hour endoscopy."

"Why didn't you tell me?"

"Farah, my dear, there's no need to tell you about things like this. It's just routine."

"I have to come back to Kuwait."

"Oh my God!" I laughed loudly. "Farah, listen to me. I'm not sick!"

I spent half an hour convincing her I was fine and that I had gone to the hospital for a simple check-up for a gastric ulcer and that the results were excellent. I told her of my decision to leave the Culture and Arts Department.

"I don't care about anything except you! If you think this will help, then just go ahead. And this new novel project, if it's bothering you then just give that up, too. I was only joking about money."

The money. When I received the advance, I decided not to touch it, to put it in a separate account. If I ended up disagreeing with Khalid, I could simply return it to him, even though Shoroq suggested paying off some of our debts to the bank.

"Pay back 5,000 dinars," she said.

"If I was going to pay anything, I'd pay 10,000."

"Better," she said.

But that morning I had gone to the Salhiya Complex, and had bought a small diamond necklace for Shoroq, a bag for

Farah, earrings for Fadia, and a belt and shoes for myself. I then went to the bank to deposit 15,000 dinars into our loan account. I called Shoroq and laughed, "The 20,000 has evaporated!"

I told her that I had deposited the full amount into the loan account, and I hid the gifts.

"Good, that's the best thing to do," she said.

I reached Khalid's house. The secretary had confirmed the time of the meeting that morning.

I didn't know why I wasn't in a better mood. I had woken up that morning uncomfortable, confused, hating everything. Had I made a mistake in agreeing to this project?

But I realized it was already too late. I had spent some of the money before even starting on the novel, so now I was committed.

There were still a few minutes before half past nine. Good. A young man came over.

"Welcome. Please …" he said.

The corridor had a mixture of smells – roses and recently cut herbs. Next time I would visit Khalid during the day so that I could see his garden. The front door opened as I reached the steps.

"Good evening," said Mai, taking me by surprise.

Standing beside her was a young woman taller than her, holding Adel's hand.

"This is my younger sister, Mona," she said with a laugh, "although she's not so young anymore! She's already in her third year at Kuwait University."

I looked at Mona's face, but it showed no signs of welcome. I put out my hand to shake hers, but she barely nodded her head. She stretched out her fingertips and mumbled in English a "hi" laden with arrogance.

I ignored her aloofness and bent over to kiss Adel.

"Where's Fadia?" he asked me.

I smiled. "Fadia's asleep now."

"Excuse me," Mona said in the same tone, then walked away with Adel. She certainly seemed upset about something.

"My father's waiting for you in the lounge," Mai said.

I stepped inside and she fell into step beside me as we passed through the main hall and came to the elevator.

I was puzzled by her sister's behavior.

It was strange, but I felt like a doctor making a house call on a patient against his will. I wondered whether Mai had told her sister I would be writing her father's life story.

The elevator door opened and Khalid appeared.

"Welcome, welcome," he said warmly. "Come in. Tonight we will sit upstairs."

Mai and I went into the elevator and up to the first floor. When the door opened, I saw a large golden-framed picture in which Khalid and Awatef were sitting in two luxurious chairs with Mai and Mona behind them and their brother Walid in the middle. I noticed that Mona was standing close to her mother.

There was a sofa suite in a muted cumin color, facing a large flat-screen TV. The polished marble floors were decorated with strips of copper and the ceiling was a dome painted as a blue sky with shining stars.

I always noticed the smells in the places I visited. My mother would always say, "Every house has its own smell. House smells reflect the family." And every woman had her own smell, too.

"This is our daily sitting area," Khalid said. He switched off the TV and called: "Mnote!"

A familiar smell came to me now. In the corner, I noticed a bouquet of white delphiniums. One of the housekeepers came in.

"What would you like to drink?"

"Tea, please."

"So, where did we finish last time?"

"Nowhere," I answered. "That is, we're still at the beginning. I opened a file on my computer and entered in all the things you've talked about so far. We stopped with your meeting with your future father-in-law."

"Ah, yes."

I felt that the walls, the smell of the flowers, and even the stars on the dome were all waiting in silence to hear Khalid's story.

"Well, I was desperate when I left my meeting with Abdul Razzaq. I realized that to be with Awatef and marry her was just a dream – maybe an impossible one. That night we talked for a long time on the phone. She was confident, though, telling me not to worry, that she was sure she could get him to agree.

"I was doubtful, though. 'What are you going to do?' I asked her.

"'It's none of your business. I am the only daughter and I know how to convince my father,' she said.

"The question ran through my head. What could she do? It was true that she was the only daughter, but it was also true that she had five brothers, and all of them opposed our marriage. Later on, I discovered she had threatened her mother that she would simply leave.

"'If my father doesn't agree, one day you'll wake up and I'll be gone. I will run away with Khalid!' she told her."

Khalid suddenly stopped and looked at me. "Awatef is a very tough woman," he said, as if to himself.

Mnote, the housekeeper, came in carrying a tea tray and put it on the table in front of us.

"I don't want to offend Awatef or her father," he said. "I won't agree to publishing anything that affects them."

I was surprised at this rather inflated fear of his wife and her family.

"I just want a small novel about my career, a novel that reveals the social harassment I faced and that I still feel."

"But you must understand that your career involves your relationship with your wife and her family," I interjected. He didn't like what I was saying, I could tell, but I continued, "Kuwait is a small place. Some people believe that Abdul Razzaq Al-Abdullatif is behind your success."

He looked intently at my face, weighing every word I said. A cloud crossed his face.

"My career is the theme of the novel, although some Kuwaiti people will continue to haunt me until I die," he continued in a strangely pained tone of voice.

I didn't know how to reply so I picked up my teacup.

Khalid simply ignored what I had said. "I will wait till the day I die to receive the miserable recognition that never comes," he said. I knew that feeling myself.

"I waited a year and a half for Abdul Razzaq's approval. Awatef, meanwhile, refused to tell me what was going on at home. She just kept saying, 'What's happening in our house concerns only us. If you love me, you have to wait.'

"But Awatef is stubborn! And thanks to her insistence and because she had her mother on her side, Abdul Razzaq changed his position and finally agreed to our marriage. But her older brother Mubarak was still against it. I'll never forget his offensive words. He said, without any respect, that he and his brothers would not agree to our marriage. Shame bites at us, doesn't it? And we don't know how to face people. He attacked me, saying,

'Thanks to you, my sister was a wily fox playing on our father's feelings. I'm sure you'll cheat on her in the end.'"

It was our third meeting and Khalid still hadn't said anything significant about his business life.

"Abdul Razzaq loves his daughter very much. He told me that she was more precious than all the money in the world, that when he agreed to our marriage, he was giving me his soul. And he was quite intimidating. He said, 'Be careful, don't upset Awatef. Otherwise my anger will pursue you.'"

I again noticed the smell of the delphiniums and looked up at the stars on the dome.

"In all my life, I will never forget Awatef's sacrifice for my sake, so I do my best to avoid upsetting her. Abdul Razzaq helped me a lot in the beginning, that's true. When I graduated from college, he hired me straight into one of his companies and put me in a good position. He showed great respect for me in front of everyone and encouraged others to follow suit. He asked me one day to visit him in his *diwaniya*. When I went in, he stood up and shook my hand in such a respectful way in front of everyone, and he welcomed me in a loud voice, sending a clear message about his relationship with me.

"I was embarrassed by his kindness and his humility. But I was aware that he was trying to create a new perception of me in a society that respects only money and wealth. I was sure he was doing everything for his daughter, of course, and probably his disproportionate interest in me showed up my weakness to others."

Khalid paused for a few seconds. Then his tone changed. "After my marriage, I noticed that my Uncle Fahad started treating me differently. He invited me to his *diwaniya* and suddenly insisted I was always 'most welcome.' He even showed new respect for my father. He let him sit next to him and he soon got into the habit of introducing me to his friends as 'Khalid, the son-in-law of Abdul Razzaq Al-Abdullatif.'

"I'm surprised these memories are nipping at me like this! I don't really know where to start. I didn't plan to tell you all this, but …"

Mnote the housekeeper came in quietly to take away the tea tray.

"The moment we became husband and wife, I embarked on a new life. Yes, marriage took me to a very new life. I started going to Abdul Razzaq's *diwaniya* every night and I listened carefully to all the conversations there. He began pushing me to make friends with the people who came to his *diwaniya* and to become one of them. He also brought me onto the boards of several large companies. He was always telling me, 'You have to know everything. Keep your eyes and ears open – don't miss anything …'

"Through Awatef, I discovered a whole new life. I remember the day she took me to buy some new suits. It was the first time I had bought Lanvin or Christian Dior, and it was the first time I had worn Bally or Moreschi shoes. And before that, she bought me a gold Rolex watch! I wish I didn't have disagreements with Awatef," he concluded with a sigh.

I hadn't expected him to speak so openly but now he had said it clearly. I had a wealth of detail for a novel, if I could use it.

The villa around us was still and silent. I was glad I had put my phone on silent mode. I had told Shoroq I would be back by twelve o'clock.

"We live in an eastern society, where men are different from women," Khalid continued. "I felt embarrassed when Awatef paid my bills, but she just laughed. 'It's my money,' she said. 'And I'm free! It brings happiness to my heart.' And I remember her words: 'If you were in my position, you would do the same. Why do Arab men have the right to spend money on the women they love while women do not have the right to do so for their husbands?' You know, more than once, she asked me bitterly how it was that if her brother Mubarak married a girl and spent all his money on her, nobody would dare stop him. Why was it allowed for men, yet forbidden for women?

"We traveled to Europe on our honeymoon – London, Paris, Spain. And for the first time, I traveled first class. At Heathrow Airport, a black Rolls Royce with a young chauffeur wearing formal dress and cap was waiting for us. He leaned over and opened the door for me with a 'Welcome, sir.' I noticed that Awatef was watching me. 'Behave as if you've ridden in Rolls your whole life,' she whispered to me.

"Everything was new to me then. For the first time, I stayed in a royal suite in a five-star hotel. In London, we walked around Harrods and the Knightsbridge shops. In Paris, I came to know the Hotel George V, Maxim's restaurant, the Champs-Élysées cafes, and the Lido cabaret dance concerts. We visited the Louvre Museum, Notre-Dame, and the Eiffel Tower. A new world opened up before me. I enjoyed Awatef's love, and her passion for pleasure and amusement made my head spin. Everything around me was new, so I tried my best to stay balanced. I lived in her happiness and in her engagement with life, but something kept nagging me. I told her I wasn't used to having such a good time. I remember how she laughed and told me to just forget about everything, just to enjoy the moment. In Europe I soon realized that I could only have these things if I was with Awatef, and that I would need to work for decades to save the kind of money I would need for such a sumptuous life. It was there that I began to notice how other Kuwaitis looked at me."

"I can't just ignore all of these details," I interrupted. He looked at me as if he had only just noticed I was there.

"Well, that's what happened," he said. "My story reflects my personal life of course, but that's something that also applies to a lot of people in Kuwait. My friend Nasser said to me, 'You married a treasure!' He told me I had kidnapped the girl that all the rich young rich men dreamed of: the poor handsome young man had married the millionaire girl!"

Khalid calmed down and allowed his breathing to slow.

"At the beginning of my career, I didn't know much," he continued, "but I did my best to learn. Abdul Razzaq was watching and following my work. The envy began soon after we were married. I started to read the annoyance in some people's eyes. For them I should have been a low-level functionary like my father until the day I died."

"Why do you care what others think?" I asked.

He paused and reached out for the glass of water. The house was silent.

"You know where the problem lies?" Khalid asked. "Everyone must remain imprisoned in his own social class." I was surprised by his admission.

"Especially in a small society like ours, no one accepts it if you rise in the social hierarchy, you see. My marriage lifted me up into a higher social class, but they couldn't accept this! This alone was enough to alienate people and provoke their petty discontent."

I saw he was having more difficulty with his breathing. I wanted to calm him down, but I didn't know how.

"You can become a millionaire, but only if you remain in the same social class and don't forget your origins. Your destiny is to bear the stamp of your class, of where you were born, even if you've moved up to join the rich at the head table."

"This is how you see it," I interjected.

"No, this is the reality!"

"I am Khalid, son of Salem, the humble civil servant. I must not forget the social class I came from. I am not allowed to compete with the sons of the rich simply because I married a millionaire's daughter. After I'd worked for years in Abdul Razzaq's companies, I resigned to start my own company with my own money. I was careful and meticulous in everything I did. Soon I expanded my operations and my company's profits increased. But the problem was ..." Khalid leaned back, wheezing. "Ah ... Let me ... rest a while."

"Of course, yes. If you feel tired, we can postpone the conversation," I said. Around me there was the smell of the flowers, the silence of the villa and the stars on the dome.

I wish Mai were here now, I thought. Where had she gone?

"My case isn't anything special in Kuwait. It's just a social fact. I marry into a rich family that has great social and economic clout, yet I remain the least part of it, whatever happens." His eyes looked sad. "You know, I spent more on Awatef than she ever spent on me. I gave her gifts dozens of times more valuable than what she gave me!" It struck me that he might be overstating the case. Surely he gave her those gifts only after she and her father had helped him to make his fortune.

Khalid continued, "But still I read the looks in some people's eyes. They don't wish me well! They point at me, and say, 'He's a parasite! A poor person shouldn't be allowed to have a place in the world of the wealthy.'"

Why did Khalid care so much what people said? It just allowed other people to interfere with his life.

"That's why I called you to write my novel." He looked at me and asked, "Do you understand what this means? It means that we, you and I, should not go beyond certain limits.

"I don't know how you're going to write these words, but when I speak about business, the picture will become clearer. It's hard. I don't know where to start and my memories overlap. What we see on the surface in any society does not reflect the reality beneath. Some people want the community to remain stratified. They don't believe in the principle of equal opportunity. Success that comes from your hard work and the fact that you have risen to the top bothers them! Everything here depends on heredity and inheritance. Wealth, social status, and prestige are the elements of success here, and everyone has to respect and obey this principle. You have to mention this issue, by the way."

Now he was giving me an order.

"What I told you here is well known to Kuwaitis," he continued. "They say it openly in the *diwaniyas*."

"But not all that's known can be written about," I pointed out.

He paused again. I glanced at the family portrait and wondered why Khalid and his wife were sitting on two separate chairs.

The marble floor, the Persian carpets, and the dome with the sky all seemed still, mired in a stony silence.

I felt thirsty. "I'd like some water, if I may," I said.

"Mnote!" Khalid called. From nowhere the maid appeared. "Some water. And arrange the dinner."

"Oh, I won't have dinner, thank you," I said.

"You must eat something with me. Mai will join us, too. We eat together almost every night."

"And Mona? I met her earlier," I asked.

"I don't think so. She will have left to take Adel to see his grandmother."

"I envy you having Mai here. My daughter Farah was also an integral part of our lives. Before she went to study in the U.S."

"And she will be again. You must miss her terribly, though."

"I do. We both do. But, well, I don't mind admitting that while Fadia is more Shoroq's 'baby girl,' perhaps because she came to us relatively late, Farah is my firstborn daughter. Nothing can ever change that."

"I understand. As Mai is mine."

We smiled at each other in silent understanding.

"How long has Mai been back living here with you?" I felt I could ask the question easily at this point, given where our discussion had led us.

"Since last year, before her divorce …"

I thought of asking him about that. I was even framing the question in my mind, but then I decided not to seem intrusive.

"Whenever I remember that evening, a sadness comes over me," he continued. "I was just drifting off to sleep when I heard Mai's voice. At first, I thought I was only imagining it, given that she wasn't living here then. But the door to my room opened and I saw her face. As a shaft of moonlight caught it, I saw she was crying. I jumped out of bed and rushed toward her.

"'What's happened?' I asked her. She choked back sobs, so I asked again, 'Mai, what's happened?' I was frightened. It was the first time I had seen her like that since she got married.

"'I, I've left him! I want to divorce him!' she said, spitting out the words. Her vehemence caught me completely by surprise. 'I won't live with a … with a drug addict!'

"I was aghast and 'Oh …' was all I could whisper in reply. I was expecting it to be just another of their usual disputes. I never for a second thought he was into drugs. Stupid, stupid.

"'For two years I've tried to make it work ... the mood swings, the anger, the ... nothing in his eyes! It's impossible to live with him ... T-tonight he ...'" She choked back more sobs.

"I was confused, still half asleep. She told me that one of his friends had come to visit. They had sat together for an hour or so before she was shocked to find her husband and him passed out with two needles on the table.

"'What?!' I demanded.

"'I almost died of fear! I-I didn't know what to do! I called an ambulance and left the house the moment it arrived.'

"'Oh Mai, my dear. I'm sorry. Come, sit,' I said. We moved over to the bed and I sat her down on the edge. I asked her how long it had been going on. She told me a year. Or maybe longer, she said.

"'I-I wanted to tell you, but ...'

"I told her it was OK, that I understood why she hadn't wanted to tell me.

"The next morning, Mai and I sat down and she talked about several of her husband's drug-related incidents. Later that morning four of my people and I went to her house. I asked my assistant to meet us there too, and she supervised moving all Mai's things back to my house – her real home."

Well, that's a story, I thought, but it's a shame I can't use it.

As Khalid took a sip of water, Mai came into the room.

"Ah, and here she is," he beamed.

"Have you been talking about me?"

"Only in the most glowing of terms, of course," Khalid assured her.

"I wonder!" Mai said with a smile at her father and walked over to put her arms around him from behind his chair.

"Tonight your father has spoken about many things," I said.

"I thought of joining you, but I wasn't sure I should. Mr. Alrefai prefers that I don't," she told her father.

Khalid looked up and behind him and smiled warmly at his daughter. "Anyway, you already know everything, and you can read the novel before it's published," he said.

"It's up to your father, of course," I said. "But we all have our own secrets that we prefer not to share with anyone."

Mai nodded. "Well, let's continue this at the table, shall we? Dinner is ready."

Khalid nodded and rose with a blank expression on his face. I followed them down to a small lounge on the ground floor, where a table had been prepared for three.

"Taleb didn't write down anything tonight. He just listened," Khalid said as we all sat down.

Mai looked at me.

"Your father is very sensitive about family information," I said.

"Family secrets," he insisted. I put a little green salad on my plate.

"By the way, I read a beautiful novel by a Japanese writer called Mishima," Khalid said.

"Which one?" I asked him.

"*Confessions of a Mask*."

"Ah, yes. It's a wonderful novel. Thoughtful, too. It affected many sections of Japanese society after World War II."

We ate for a while and made small talk about this and that, nothing much. Suddenly Khalid stopped eating.

"I'm sorry, but I think I've had enough," he said.

Mai looked alarmed. "Are you tired?" she asked.

"No."

I stopped eating too.

"No, go ahead, please," Khalid said.

Trying to change the subject, I asked him how many times he thought we would need to sit down together.

"Four or five, I would say. I'll talk about business and the endless aggravations."

Mai looked seriously anguished and none of us spoke. I thought it might be best to leave them together. I didn't want to overstay my welcome. I put my fork down on the plate and said, "Forgive me, would you? I really should go. Shoroq can't sleep until I get home and she's not been well today."

"Of course," Khalid said. "Nothing serious, I hope?"

"Oh no. A little worn down, that's all. The doctor told her to take a few vitamin and mineral supplements. She'll be fine. Thank you for asking."

"Wish her well from us, please," said Mai. "I hope we'll be getting together with the children soon."

"She'd like that, yes. Fadia keeps asking about Adel now!"

"I'll call you and we can agree on the next meeting," Khalid said as I rose. "There's a lot of information I've yet to talk about."

"I'll need some time to write down what we've talked about tonight. It's not that I'll write the specifics, of course," I added when I caught Khalid's expression. "I could, for example, raise the issues of class segregation from a narrative point of view, the author questioning the rights and wrongs of the things you talked about."

Khalid nodded. "Mmm. I see. I'll say good night from here if I may."

He stayed seated at the dining room table as Mai walked with me. I could sense her anxiety.

"Has my father said anything to you about his illness?" she asked when we were out of earshot of her father.

"No, nothing at all. But then, perhaps he wouldn't. We aren't 'friends' in the strict sense."

"Oh, Mr. Alrefai, you *are* his friend – don't doubt that. And mine, too, I hope?"

I nodded and smiled at this innocent, yet very sharp, young lady.

"This novel will bind you together. Bind us all together, I think. That is, you and my father and I. Dad is always sad," Mai said, speaking more as a worried daughter than as a businesswoman and mother. "Of course, he covers it up. Possibly it even goes away sometimes when he's playing with Adel."

It was not only the writer in me that picked up on this opening. I had come to genuinely care. And now Mai was saying they were my friends. Maybe there was some truth in what she said.

"Why is he sad?" I asked. "That is, if you don't mind me asking?" I added quickly, just in case I sounded too intrusive.

We came to the door and our eyes met.

"Let me walk you to your car," she said, as if announcing a decision she had already taken.

We walked out into the cool night air, with only the sounds of nature for company – the light breeze in the trees, a few insects droning in the night. A bird or two fluttered in the distance. I waited for Mai to say something as we walked.

"After my divorce," she began, "when I came to live with my father, I soon began to realize the misery his life had become. A 60-year-old man living alone in a silent house with just the walls, the maids, a driver, and a gardener for company. A man speaking to himself most of the time, filling the space with sadness.

"Dad gets up early, drinks his coffee while reading the newspapers silently, then returns to his room, takes a shower, dresses, and leaves the house for the office. No fun in his day – just work and only work! What happiness can money offer a man who's fed up with his own gloomy thoughts?

"I make sure to wake up early to have breakfast with him and try to brighten up his morning. We talk about the news, novels we've read, and movies we've seen. Adel will join us most days, if he hasn't been too active the day before and isn't too tired. I want Dad's days to begin with sweetness and light. And to remind him there is something bright to come home to."

When we reached my car, I was in no hurry to take out my keys.

Mai looked down, then up at the trees nearby. "He told me once, 'Your mother began this separation. She was always consumed by her family.'

"For her part, my mother said he had dark obsessions that he seemed happy to endure, that she could never change him and that, in the end, she couldn't live with him. Having lived with her for so many years, I knew her well. I knew how much effort she really did make. And now that I'm a divorced woman who's tasted the cruelty of men, I understand how much it takes to separate a wife from her husband. But I also realized who did and who didn't deserve most of the blame, and it wasn't my father. My dear father. I understand him and I only want to help him, to bring a few smiles to his face."

She sighed. Poor Mai, I thought. "I see," I said. "Do you think it's these events that have brought out …" I hesitated, not knowing how much Khalid had told his daughter about his issues with class and acceptance, "brought out his worries about how he's viewed by others in business?"

"Maybe. I thought this novel … I thought it would be something positive, a way for him to see all he's accomplished by looking back on his life. Where he came from, where he is now. What he's done for us, his family. I never thought my mother would object so strongly. I thought, and hoped, she would see that and contribute. Perhaps she will see that at least, even if she doesn't contribute." Mai looked away, focusing on nothing I could see.

"I wish I could help him," I said, not only to break the silence.

"You will. You *are*,' she said, turning back to me.

"Well, I'm delighted to be your friend and to try to bring your father some kind of happiness."

"Thank you. I think the novel will make him happy. Once we get past this awkwardness."

"I will do my best."

"I know you will, Mr. Alrefai. And I thank you for it. And so will Dad when it's finished, even if it doesn't seem that way now."

I nodded and smiled. "Well, good night then."

"And to you."

I got in my car and, as I drove away, looked up to the dark sky, hoping for the faint sparkle of a star – any star.

Chapter 7

Thursday, May 3, 2007

Three days after our last meeting, Khalid took me by surprise by calling at half past eight in the morning.

"Good morning," he said. He sounded worried. "Can we meet this evening?"

The request was also a surprise. It was a holiday and my large family had agreed to gather at my house.

"If necessary I could," I said tactfully.

"I'll be waiting for you at half past eight then, at home."

"Who was that?" Shoroq asked me. She was sitting by my side, reading the newspaper.

"Khalid."

"What did he want?"

"To see me tonight."

I wanted to ask him if there was anything wrong. I wondered why he had called. I was thinking how I was not a writer on permanent call, and then Khalid called me back.

"There's nothing to worry about," he said. "It's just that I'd like to continue our conversation."

"OK then," I agreed.

"Are you are going to go?" Shoroq asked after the second call.

"Yes."

"You shouldn't."

"We have a contract and I have to keep to it," I said, although we had already agreed on that evening for the family gathering.

"A contract to write a novel, not to work to order at his whim whenever he wants you. Why didn't say you couldn't make it?"

Shoroq just looked at me.

"This is the first time Khalid has called me like this," I said.

"Thursday night is family night. How could you abandon everyone?"

She was right, I knew.

I left her and went downstairs to hide in my office on the ground floor, where I turned on the computer to review everything Khalid had said at our last meeting.

I started to think about everything we had talked about. According to Khalid's plan, it would still be four or five meetings, but so far he hadn't talked about any work issues. He didn't want me to say anything about his family life, but he didn't talk about anything else.

***

Traffic was light, so when I reached Khalid's house it was only twenty-five past eight. The place was very quiet. I didn't know why he had been in such a hurry to set up this meeting.

A young man was waiting for me out front. He greeted me and told me we would be going to the lower floor.

We went downstairs. Wonderful garden smells greeted me as I walked along the garden paths, dim lights guiding our steps. There were parts of the garden I hadn't seen before and in the right-hand corner there was a small swimming pool. The young man walked me over to a lounge separated from the garden by a glass façade. The door opened the moment we arrived and Khalid appeared.

"You're certainly punctual about your appointments," he said.

The lighting was rather dim inside.

Khalid was wearing a *dishdasha*, but with his head uncovered. He was not alone.

"Nasser Alnasser," said Khalid, introducing me to his friend, the former minister. "Taleb Alrefai, the writer." Nasser, wearing the traditional headdress, got up and offered his hand. "Hello," he said.

"Hello," I replied.

"Excuse me, but I have to go," he added, a sharp look in his eyes.

"Stay with us a while," pleaded Khalid.

"I really can't," he said. He sounded upset to have met me.

He looked straight at me and went aggressively to the point. "How are you going to set about writing this 'novel'?" he asked.

His question took me aback. I looked at him for a moment and said, "I'm not sure yet."

"I advised Khalid to forget about it," he continued. "We are not used to such books in Kuwait, as you know. I wish you would reconsider writing it."

His meddling surprised me. "I think this is between Mr. Khalifa and me," I said.

He ignored my reply. "It is not appropriate to disclose family secrets for money!" he declared.

On the defensive, I ignored him and looked toward Khalid. I was trying to stay calm, though inside I was fuming.

"Would you write your own biography?" he asked.

"Some day, perhaps," I ventured. I wanted to say that most of what I wrote was a part of my life, but I felt that he would not appreciate the value of that.

The man genuinely appeared to hate me, though this was the first time we had met.

"In the West they call this 'confessional literature,'" he told me. "Writers and celebrities confess the secrets of their personal lives, of their relationships with women! But a businessman's life is traveling, meetings, money transactions, and profit. What do you intend to write about Khalid?"

His question annoyed me, since it was a form of direct interference in the contract between Khalid and me. But I refused to be drawn and Khalid held his peace too.

"I know a lot of secrets about Khalid," Nasser added, addressing me directly.

"Good for you," I said.

He didn't like my answer. "Goodbye," he said curtly.

"Bye," said Khalid, as I silently wished him good riddance.

He walked off and Khalid followed, so I sat down to recover from this bizarre encounter.

There were two glasses on the table, together with a bottle of Bordeaux red wine, a bottle of Chivas Regal, a small bucket of ice, a bottle of mineral water and a few snacks – nuts and potato chips, fresh vegetables, and a plate of cheeses.

A lovely blend of garden fragrances filled the room. I knew I was there for the money and reminded myself that necessity could humble a man.

"Welcome," said Khalid as he reappeared. "Nasser is my best friend. He's a bold man but his tongue can sometimes be hurtful."

Our eyes met. "I don't like him," I admitted.

"Well, I can understand that. Would you like some wine, some whisky, vodka?"

"Water or 7Up would be fine."

"Would you like a beer perhaps?"

"No, thank you. I don't drink alcohol."

Khalid opened a decorative wooden door by pushing the two leaves apart. A large semi-circular wooden bar made of reddish brown mahogany appeared, lit with bright lights. The bar was full of alcoholic drinks and crystal glasses of various kinds.

"This bar was designed by a famous Italian architect," Khalid explained. "Since alcoholic drinks are forbidden in restaurants and hotels in Kuwait, I like to celebrate with my guests and my friends here. I know a dealer who brings me the finest wines and all kinds of spirits. I order a buffet dinner and service from five-star hotels, and then we have a lovely time around the pool in the garden until early morning. Why don't you try a Bordeaux wine?"

"No, thanks. Really."

He brought me over a can of 7Up, and as soon as he was seated, he said, "Sorry, maybe I called you here at a bad time. But I felt we had to meet." He poured a little wine for himself and raised the glass. "Cheers."

I raised my 7Up and smiled. "Cheers."

"We are friends now, so I'll call you Taleb and you'll call me Khalid. You know, after our last meeting, I found myself rather sunk in ideas and obsessions, in memories and fears, so that's why I wanted to meet tonight.

"Nasser is rather contemptuous of this novel idea, and annoyed by it too. He asked me to put a stop to it, but I told him it would be about my experience in business and nothing else. But he said, 'We're in Kuwait, not in Sweden or America,' which did put me on my guard, I must confess. It could turn into a scandal and it might be a fertile field for rumors and misinterpretations."

Khalid was waiting for me to respond, but I didn't, so he continued, "Nasser thinks I'm perhaps harming myself and my family, and certainly Awatef's family. He reminded me that Kuwait's a small place and nothing stays secret."

"Well, it's your decision, of course."

"Yes, yes. I think Nasser is being contradictory, though. He sees the novel as a scandal but says that nothing stays secret in Kuwait. So if the people of Kuwait know your story, then where is the scandal?"

"I hope you don't misunderstand me," I said, weighing my words carefully, "as I am keen to write the novel. But I do see a clear contradiction."

He nodded and took a sip from his glass.

"You write the novel, and in the end I will decide what to do," he finally resolved.

"This means I would write the novel but you might decide not to publish it?" I retorted, slightly alarmed at the prospect.

"Maybe. I don't know."

I didn't know what to say, though I felt upset at the idea.

"Nasser told me that Awatef's brother Mubarak had asked him to persuade me to forget about the idea. But I've made my decision and I'm not going back on it." He took a sip of wine. "Since I married Awatef, Mubarak has never spoken to me. If we ever meet by chance, he completely ignores me." He looked up. "Please, this is not for publication."

Oh my God, this is getting ridiculous, I thought. He kept telling me things and then saying they were not for publication.

"As I said before, please make sure you avoid writing about my family secrets and my relationship with my wife, especially as Awatef is against the novel." He held his wine glass and looked into empty space.

"The contract is between you and me and so no one else should interfere," I said.

"It isn't just what you think. It's much more complicated than a simple contract for a novel. But I'm still convinced of the idea of the novel, though I need you to be careful."

"Perhaps you're making too much of it. You can be sure not all Kuwaitis will read the novel."

"A novel that features real names? Believe me, everyone will look out for it." He picked up his glass. "Are you sure you don't want to try the wine?"

"Yes, I'm sure," I said with a smile. "Thank you, though." The faint lights cast shadows of fatigue over Khalid's face and eyes.

"I loved Awatef and she loved me," he said. "But society resented our relationship and our marriage. I remember very clearly when my brother Saleh advised me not to marry her and said that even if I married into a family of high status, I would still be the poor man and they the rich. It would be like wearing clothes that are too long for you and that make you trip up. And I remember too the night of our marriage celebration for men: the difference between my family and Awatef's family. I felt then how money could plant evil thoughts in some people's hearts. It can make them puff up their chests with pride and look down on others with scorn."

It was strange how Khalid talked about the rich as if he were not one of them.

Khalid poured himself some more wine and sipped it appreciatively. "Every society makes up its own narratives, whether true or false," he said. "When people spread these narratives, they become a powerful presence. They solidify into truth.

"After we got married, Awatef's mother gave us a villa. I objected but she said it was for her daughter. Of course, I didn't have the money to buy a villa at the time, so I agreed." He stopped and looked at me. "You know, nothing is for free; you take a tax break now and it will actually cost you more in the long run than simply paying the tax. This became the pattern in my relationship with Awatef and her family. The day I accepted the villa, I opened a door I couldn't close."

He reached for a piece of cheese and said with a smile, "You can eat, please. Eating is not forbidden here!"

I smiled back and took a piece of carrot.

"Awatef secretly opened a bank account in my name and made a deposit. 'This way, as far as everyone else is concerned, it will be you who furnishes the villa,' she said. I wasn't happy about it but she questioned how else we could furnish our home. She reminded me that we were husband and wife now, that this was our home.

"By the way, her mother visited us in our villa only once and none of her brothers ever did. The early days of our marriage were hard. I was tense and I ignored the dilemma I'd put myself in. It was difficult for me to cope with Awatef and her family and difficult to stay out of their way. I was tense all the time. I felt like everyone had their eyes on me."

This was the Khalid of my novel, the narrator. This was clearly his life story. I could see the fatigue in his eyes and in the way he spoke, though, and again he was breathing with some difficulty.

"There's one thing I remember as if it happened yesterday. Once I said to Awatef that we shouldn't have married. She looked at me and started crying. I always hate myself when I'm tough with her. She said, 'I love you and I can't live without you. I stood up to my family for you. Don't ruin our lives now!'

"I was confused. I didn't know what to do. Awatef was the love of my life. It wasn't her fault that her family was rich. But I didn't have enough money to spend on her and she didn't want to live a life of deprivation when she had money. I had to choose – either I accepted my new life or we would get divorced. So I accepted living in the villa. And the bank account. But I was like someone who was still looking for his old clothes while wearing the new.

"I remember when I visited my mother one day. We were sitting waiting for my father to arrive when a strange smile appeared on her face. 'So this is the new Khalid,' she said. 'You've changed. You don't come to visit me unless I call you.' She was upset; she told me she didn't blame my wife but me. 'I heard that she is pregnant, but still I haven't seen her," she said. She told me how happy she was for me but begged me not to change the way I was with our family.

"That night I felt like I'd somehow lost them – my family. But I stayed and had dinner with them. When I was leaving, my mother's words were still echoing in my head. Had I changed that much? If my family had noticed, what about other people? That night I drove down to the sea to face the silence and darkness and suddenly I found myself crying.

"The paradoxes of life are strange, aren't they? People around me were envious of me, yet I was in torment. A single question kept running through my mind: What did Awatef think of the man who was living off her money? She told me it was all in my head, that no one was saying she was wasting her money on me. 'You have your own job and your own salary,' she said. Whenever I talked about it, she said, 'Husbands and wives everywhere work together in life.'

"But in human relations, little things build up. I married Awatef, the millionaire girl. I had my honeymoon at her expense. I lived in her mother's villa. Her father hired me in one of his companies. I became one of his *diwaniya* friends. Little by little, people started looking at me as the Abdullatif family protégé.

"My relationship with my family did change. I remember when I invited my sister to visit us. Her reply was, 'Thanks, but when your wife invites us we will come.'

"Awatef loved me, yes. But on the other hand, she didn't do anything to make contact with my family. She told me more than once, 'Don't force me to do something I don't want to do.' I asked her if there was anything amiss between her and my mother and sisters. She said no. My mother, whenever I visited her, would ask, 'Where is your wife? Why doesn't she come with you?' My brother Saleh said there was a chasm of wealth that separated them from Awatef's family.

"So I was forced to persuade Awatef to visit my family. But she was so reluctant to speak it was like she wore a mask. Their relationship was stillborn. In human emotions, things that are unspoken matter. They work in silence – more so than any words. Awatef's behavior made my mother and sisters begin to avoid her. Yes, human relations live through the chemistry between people, not through what they say outwardly."

Khalid took another sip of his wine. "My situation at that time was really difficult," he continued.

"Every day I was pulled away from my own family and dragged into the world of the Abdullatif family. After working in his company for a while, I began to learn how money makes money. I remember one particular incident. I was following up on a big contract with one of the ministries. After winning the project, the company had to submit a bank guarantee for more than 500,000 dinars to the ministry. I was working to secure the money for the bank guarantee. Abdul Razzaq passed by my office one morning and asked about the project. I explained to him that I was trying to secure the money so that the bank would issue the guarantee and then we could get payment from the ministry. He looked at me, at my naivety, and told me just to call the bank manager. He had already spoken with the manager and the manager had agreed to issue the bank guarantee the same day without any security from our company. Before Abdul Razzaq left my office, he whispered to me, 'We are the Abdullatif Company. We get bank guarantees and facilities without any cover because we are strong.' It was that day I fully realized how Abdul Razzaq's name could open any door and that rules applied only to the weak and the poor. That day I understood that rules could be kneaded like dough in the hands of powerful people."

"Can I mention this incident?" I asked.

"Please, don't say anything about Abdul Razzaq and his family." So he called me because he just needs to talk, I thought. But maybe I could include the incident in the book if I disguised some of the details.

"Suddenly, I was an excited young man in a new environment," he continued. "Awatef started working in a bank and then founded her own company, and soon she started to manage some big contracts and was busy with work all the time. We were living in the same house, but in our own worlds. We would maybe meet for a meal and talk about how our day had been. By then I had left Abdul Razzaq's company and had founded my own company.

"You know, I didn't expect to reveal my life story to anybody. I never thought it would be so clear in my mind. I didn't tell you before what really bothers me more than anything. Well, it's the perception of inferiority I read in people's eyes, and later on the conflict with Awatef."

Khalid was so eager to talk I didn't even need to prompt him any longer.

"As I told you, I founded my own enterprise. Nasser had given me a nickname, 'lucky man,' although I wasn't keen on sharing that with anyone except my children. Anyway, I started to make money and build up a reputation in business. But still many people were adamant that I was taking advantage of Abdul Razzaq's money and prestige. I was hurt that they judged me so unfairly. They insisted on treating me as a poor young man, the son of a junior civil servant. They refused to see me as Khalid the respectable businessman!"

He paused for a few seconds and took a deep breath. Looking at his wineglass, he said, "There are people who feel they are better than others for no reason. At every turn they remind a man of his humble origins, as if they're taking some kind of revenge on him! There was another incident I'll never forget. I had gone to my friend's weekly *diwaniya* one day when I heard one of them say, 'Khalid's a thief! He became a millionaire by climbing on the shoulders of his wife's company.' And I remember the look of panic on his face the moment we locked eyes. I just stood in the doorway looking at him. His face changed color and he started to stammer. 'Please come in, have a seat,' another friend said.

"I ignored the invitation and challenged all of them. 'Anyone can amass a fortune,' I said. 'But you cannot buy honor! You say I'm a thief? Then I say you're a son of a bitch. Stand up and face me if that's not the case!'

"Many of my *diwaniya* 'friends' came over to me and begged me to calm down, said they were sorry, but that night I was ready to fight anyone! I refused to sit in the *diwaniya*. I told them, 'You're all like sick men gathered here! I will not sit with you. Die of your petty jealousy and anger! My ambition knows no bounds.' And I left, my heart full of sadness. And that was the last time I ever went to a *diwaniya*."

Khalid took a long sip of his wine. "After I heard what my friends in the *diwaniya* said about me," he continued, "I saw for myself that in every society there are levels. Each level fights desperately to defend itself and tries to stop strangers from intruding. The upper classes will gladly expel any newcomer! Oh, they might possibly accept him as rich or he might be promoted in government. He might even be called a friend, but he can never be accepted as a member of their class. Water doesn't mix with oil, even if it's in the same pot. There are always those who believe that human beings should live apart." He struggled to talk between short breaths. "The others will never accept you in their kingdom. Abandon any hope of that. You understand me, yes?"

"Yes, I understand." His pain certainly seemed to be genuine.

"You know, there are people who take pleasure in defaming people's honor."

I couldn't help it, but I was moved by what he said.

"I always wonder," he continued, "if I hadn't married Awatef but had still became a millionaire, would I have suffered in the same way? The estrangement from Awatef has hurt me a lot. Day by day, little by little, our love wilted. Maybe she realized she had made a mistake and regretted it, or maybe people's looks whittled away at her love for me. Anyway, Awatef drifted away from me. She was busy with her work and travel, and she let me drown in my own worry and pain. More than once I asked her why she was avoiding me. Each time, she came up with the same answer: 'You're imagining it.'

"I think the bitter truth is that we were beginning to live the differences between us after marriage, and we discovered that we didn't know how to change. We would argue and sleep on our disputes, and in the morning, each of us would run off to take refuge in our own work. Every day we grew farther apart. We lived for years with nothing in common but the term 'husband and wife.' We travelled together, but we slept in separate rooms and we met in the morning around a dining table. I'm sorry about this," he said, looking up at me with sad eyes. "It's a painful story to tell."

I didn't know how to answer.

"It's amazing, isn't it," he continued, "how love dies. Awatef has always been self-sufficient. She doesn't rely on anyone. She knows many people but she doesn't really have people you could call friends. She always looks down on others, considers them somehow beneath her. I've told her repeatedly about her not feeling empathy for others."

Khalid broke off and looked at me, then continued. "I hope you understand. I don't want to criticize Awatef, but sometimes I feel that my marriage and my life with her created the 'me' that I am now. Awatef is a tough person to deal with. She could never bear hearing these things from me. She would think they were just attacks on her. Love disguises our defects, but when it starts to wane, the hate hormone is activated and that brings out the deficiencies in us all. But still, you can't write anything against Awatef."

Poor Khalid. He has an Awatef complex, I thought.

"I'm sure you've noticed I live without my wife," Khalid continued. "Awatef lives with Mona in her father's house. Abdul Razzaq's illness was the final straw in our relationship. The obsession bugged me for years. I always worried that Awatef was just waiting for the right opportunity to leave me. When her father fell ill, she started to visit him daily, then she began to spend the night with him, and finally moved in to live with him."

The wine bottle was almost empty as Khalid continued his story.

"I discussed it with her but she just said, 'I can't leave my father! No man can ever replace my father.'

"'What about me?' I asked her.

"'We'll see each other all the time, and you can come to my father's house whenever you want,' she said.

"Mai and her son have given me meaning in life. She has lived with me since she left her home after her divorce from her addict husband. I feel sorry for her, though. Maybe I just needed somebody to tell my sad story to," he said with a sigh. "You know, Taleb, most psychotherapy is based on talking out what's in your heart, revealing and reliving your pain. People see me from the outside. They see the false face: Khalid the millionaire, Khalid the son-in-law of Abdul Razzaq, Khalid the man who can get whatever he wants. Nobody knows anything about my real life. No one lives with my suffering. Money doesn't bring happiness at all. It didn't take me long to discover that. Or that God spreads crumbs of happiness among humans equally. Everyone can have their share, at least for a time."

Khalid suddenly stopped talking and looked at me.

"Do you mind if I ask you something?" he asked.

"Of course not."

"Do you have a 'special' relationship with any women?"

His question took me by surprise.

"I mean, you're a well-known writer, a novelist, so you must have admirers who pursue you. I was wondering if maybe you have a special friend, a secret relationship with a woman that Shoroq doesn't know anything about."

"No," I replied.

"Of course. It's just that we are men, after all. And both of us successful and well known in our fields. And women like prominent, successful men. I'm sure you know that there are many apartments where men meet beautiful women for good times, drinking, singing, dancing, sex. Several of my friends keep apartments for fun with women. They've asked me if I wanted to use their apartments but I've always refused. Once, though, I did go to visit a friend in his apartment after he insisted several times. I arrived at half past eight, I recall. The apartment had a large window overlooking the sea. There was a large lounge with a luxurious sofa, a dining table for four people, a drinks cabinet, and a large-screen TV. My friend told me he would use the place once or twice a week for fun, to forget about the pressures of work.

"The place seemed quiet. He offered me a drink. 'I have nearly everything, so what would you like?' I asked for a whisky and sat talking with him while waiting to see what would happen.

"At nine o'clock the doorbell rang and two girls came in. Both were young, in their mid-twenties, and both were gorgeous, stunning. They greeted us and sat down with us. A young man appeared – he must have been in the kitchen – and poured three more whiskies. I had another. Then he brought out some appetizers and put them on the table. I couldn't help but glance at the girls. Their sexy bodies, their soft voices, their infectious laughter, and their flirtatious looks …

"My friend pointed to one of them. 'Yasmeen is my special girl,' he said. I understood he was making sure I stayed away from that girl, so I just smiled and said OK. The other girl, Fatma, was equally gorgeous, even more so, I would say.

"While we were chatting, I noticed that Fatma was looking at me with interest. So, to live the moment, I did the same. My friend had organized dinner delivered from a well-known restaurant, which the hired help had now laid out. The moment we got up to go to the dining table, Fatma put out her hand to hold mine. 'You sit beside me,' she said. It was almost an order and I obeyed.

"The moment we sat down she said to me, 'You're rather quiet.'

"I smiled at her and said, 'Yes.'

"'We're here to have fun so relax, talk, have fun!'

"'Khalid is a man of few words, but he is very practical,' my friend said.

"She laughed loudly, and said, 'Well, I'll see for myself.'

"After dinner, my friend put on some Arabic music and the two girls got up to dance. We soon joined them. The whisky I had drunk and the atmosphere soon helped me to shed my inhibitions.

"Fatma pulled at my hand, but I held back. 'I'm enjoying dancing with you but nothing else right now,' I told her.

"My friend called me over and said, 'The girl wants you. There's a clean room ready for you if you want her.'

"At about twelve, after a lot of dancing and drinking, my friend took his girl to his room. My girl, Fatma, took my hand. 'I know the way,' she said simply and took me to the second room, where she began to take off her clothes. She swayed a little as she did so. I wondered whether it was from the music still playing or from the drink.

"'My girlfriend gets money from your friend, but I don't want your money,' she said. 'I just want us to enjoy the night together.'

"I didn't take off my clothes. She was standing in front of me topless, wearing only her little panties.

"Can you believe it?" Khalid suddenly asked me. I didn't understand his question.

"I had the sense that Awatef was with us, standing in front of me, more real to me than that miserable girl! I told the girl to put her clothes back on. She was shocked. I doubt she was used to rejection, so I tried to explain: 'You are beautiful and gorgeous, but I ...' I couldn't even say it as I noticed her looking at me with numbness in her eyes. I simply said, 'I can't.'

"I left her naked in the room and, without telling my friend, I left the apartment feeling sick. When I reached my car, I sat there for about half an hour before I dared go home. I thought that somehow Awatef would know. Men are men, after all. How could she believe I didn't stray, that she was with me even then? Awatef and our love haunt me, grab at me, even when she is cold to me. Even now. You're not drinking."

"Oh. I'm fine, thank you. I've drunk enough tonight," I replied.

He looked at me, understanding the meaning behind my reply.

"We'll meet again next week, yes?"

"OK."

"I'm sorry. I know I've disturbed you tonight. Perhaps I talked about things that have nothing to do with the novel, but I needed your help. Awatef thinks I want to write this novel to get some kind of revenge on her. Last time she came here to ask for a divorce, I told her we were already separated, each of us living our own life and so there was no need for divorce. But I felt there was something mysterious behind her request. Let me tell you something. When a man is forced to divorce the woman he loves, that means he's cutting out a piece of his heart and throwing it to the dogs. If I ever thought about taking revenge on Awatef, that would mean I was killing myself."

Khalid rose and so did I.

"Next time I will tell you about my experiences in business and the markets. Thanks for coming tonight."

"My pleasure."

He said goodbye standing near the entrance to the lounge, holding the wineglass that had become his crutch.

The garden's smells came with me as I left. I wished I didn't have to leave Khalid alone. Poor Khalid, I thought, it can't be much fun living in misery in a mansion.

Chapter 8

Monday, May 7, 2007

"Please, have a seat," said Awatef's secretary. "I'll be with you right away. Please just give me a minute, if you could."

"Of course. Take your time, please." I had received a call from Mai the day before.

"Sorry, my father sends his apologies but he can't meet you tonight."

We had agreed to meet on Sunday evening. I had already typed my notes from our last meeting into the computer and I was looking forward to the next meeting.

"He's tired, you see," Mai added.

"I hope everything is OK?"

A pause. "Well, Dad has heart problems. The doctor has told him to stop drinking alcohol and warned him about too much stress."

"Really? I'm sorry to hear that. Last time he did drink some wine."

"Yes, generally he drinks a lot. I'm scared."

"I hope things will be OK," I replied.

"I hope so too. Only …" I could hear her crying. "This is the first time he's been honest about his chest pains."

"Have you seen the doctor?"

"I tried to get him to, but he refused. I'm scared. I feel he's hiding something."

"Perhaps he just got tired from our last meeting," I suggested.

"I don't think so. On Friday morning he was happy. I went out with him and Adel for lunch. But then ..." Her voice suddenly faltered and I could hear her crying.

"Mai, what happened?"

"My mom is against the novel. Which you know. My sister Mona, she told Mom about your visit with Dad. Yesterday evening, Mom came over and asked Dad to abandon the novel." The crying returned. "She was really angry about it. And Mona hates the idea of an author writing a novel about her parents' relationship. She believes you're weaving some kind of plot against our mother."

"Can I do anything?" I might have to face Awatef, I thought.

"Thanks, but ... Look, Dad will call you later to arrange a new date, OK?"

"Of course, yes. Mai, I hope everything will be OK. I'm sure it will be."

***

"Please." The tea boy's voice startled me as he put some tea in front of me.

I was back at Awatef's office.

"My name is Magdi," her secretary said. "My apologies, but Mrs. Awatef had to attend an urgent meeting moments before you arrived. She will see you as soon as it ends."

I nodded. Magdi had called me the evening before to say that Awatef wanted to meet me. "In her office on Monday morning, say ten o'clock?" Magdi proposed.

Something bothered me, though: Where had they gotten my mobile phone number?

"Is that a good time for you?"

"Sorry, but I don't think I can," I said.

"Mrs. Awatef would prefer the meeting not to be delayed."

He insisted I take his phone number. In truth, I was free Monday morning, but something made me hesitant to go.

An hour later the secretary called me back, and after some thought, I agreed.

I thought about calling Khalid to tell him I was going to meet his wife, but I feared this would upset him or cause him anxiety that might affect his health. I thought about calling Mai, but I hesitated again, not wanting to put her in the middle.

When the secretary told me about the urgent meeting, I was annoyed. I considered leaving but decided against it, on the grounds that it would be a good opportunity to see Khalid's wife and hear her side of the story.

Other than my impressions of Awatef from Khalid, all I knew was what my friend Suleiman had told me – that she was sharp-tongued and was widely known not to have many true friends. I very much hoped her meeting would end soon, as I didn't like to wait, especially since it was they who had called me.

Awatef probably wanted to unsettle me before we met.

Magdi was busy arranging a stack of papers in front of him. It was twenty minutes to eleven. I would wait until eleven.

Farah took after me when it came to hating to wait.

"I hate all this waiting," she had said to me that day in her regular morning call. "I'm just dreaming of leaving Boulder and going home to Kuwait. I mean, everything is excellent here. It's just the homesickness. I live with these walls for company and their silence is so harsh."

"Why do you make it so hard on yourself?" I asked her.

"I don't know. I don't like it. It's the pain of separation. Perhaps it's because I'm so attached to you, Daddy!"

"Would you like some coffee perhaps?" the coffee boy asked me.

"Thank you, but no."

"I do apologize," Magdi said. "As I said, Mrs. Awatef began her meeting right before you arrived."

I didn't entirely believe him.

"When will she finish?" I asked.

"She shouldn't be long, God willing."

"Please tell her that I have another meeting at twelve."

"Of course."

I wondered whether Khalid was telling the truth about the rift between them. There was certainly something about the relationship that made him very unhappy.

***

The evening before, Shoroq, Fadia, and I had gone to visit Suleiman and Samar, and Suleiman had told me that Samar was much happier now. She was cheerful and joked with Fadia about how they would take her with them when they went abroad.

"But I have school and I don't want to travel," Fadia objected.

"Oh, your father will organize some time off for you," Samar continued jokingly.

"I don't want to, though!" said Fadia. She pulled herself off Samar's lap and ran over to Shoroq. "I'm going to stay with Mama!"

Samar got up to bring her back, smiling her warm smile. "Sweetie, I'm sorry. I'm just joking with you."

"We're leaving tomorrow morning, and the day after tomorrow Samar will begin the tests," Suleiman told me.

"I wish her well," I said.

"I'll then come back while Samar stays at the hospital till the treatment's over."

"Why don't you stay with her?"

He didn't answer me. What was it that marriage did to the hearts of men and women? How did it erode their enthusiasm for each other?

"Mrs. Awatef will meet you now," Magdi said, startling me slightly.

The door opened and Mona was standing there. "My mother has now ended her meeting," she announced. She already looked annoyed and I was very much starting to dislike the place.

"This way please," Magdi said, coming out from behind his desk to show me the way. He led me into a large room with a meeting table for six. At the back of the room Awatef was sitting behind her desk. Mona moved to sit beside her. I was surprised to see no signs of the meeting that had supposedly just ended.

"Good morning," I said.

Awatef got up and greeted me with a handshake that was somewhat perfunctory. "Have a seat, please." She gestured to a seat in front of her. "Coffee or tea?"

"Nothing, thank you."

Her sharp features suggested a certain sternness. Her pictures in the newspapers made her look smaller than she was in reality. She was wearing a necklace with large diamonds and earrings and a diamond Chopard watch on her wrist. A large oil portrait of her father hung behind her.

"I'm sorry I kept you waiting," she said.

"That's OK."

"I will be direct. Khalid told me you're writing a book about him. I want to know what you will focus on."

Mona looked on malevolently, making me reluctant to say more than I needed to say.

"I haven't actually written anything yet," I said.

"But you will be writing about my husband?"

"There is a contract between Mr. Khalifa and myself, yes."

"A 100,000 dinar contract, I understand," she said, almost openly hostile.

"May I ask what it is you require from me?"

"It's very simple," she said. "I don't want you to write about me or my family. Mr. Alrefai, you are a Kuwaiti writer and you know the nature of this society. Publishing the secrets of large families is just not done."

"That's not what the book is about," I said. "There is a contract between Mr. Khalid and myself to write his biography, yes, but he has insisted that I not write anything about you or your family."

"Really?" she said. "Would you let someone come into your house, make off with your life secrets and write a scandalous book about you and your family?"

"As I've indicated, there won't be any scandal, I assure you."

"Writing it is a scandal," she said sharply. "I consider any writing about me or my family as a disrespectful intrusion on our privacy. I intend to have this contract cancelled."

"Mr. Khalifa alone has the right to suspend or cancel our contract."

"I met with him yesterday and told him to cancel it."

"If Mr. Khalifa asks me to stop, then ..." I said.

"This isn't only about Khalid! You have no right to exploit my husband's psychological state and benefit from it by writing about us."

Although her tone was overtly hostile, I didn't respond.

"I understand your need for money. I realize 100,000 dinars is a lot to you no doubt, but nothing should tarnish the reputation of the families of Kuwait."

At that point I'd had enough. "I will not allow you to speak to me like this!" I objected.

"Stay away from my husband then."

"You're talking about your husband as if he were a child."

"Know your place!" she shouted at me, her face strained.

"Excuse me," I said and got up.

"We've not yet finished our meeting!"

I came here voluntarily, I thought, and I will not allow anyone to insult me.

We locked eyes. Surprisingly, she said, "Sorry." I sat down again and tried to calm down.

"Look, put yourself in my place," Awatef continued, forcing herself, I was sure, to be more conciliatory. "You are from a respectable family. I think you wouldn't lie down and let anyone spread scandalous stories about you either."

"There is no question of anyone being insulted or defamed," I insisted. "Mr. Khalifa has asked me repeatedly to keep his private life out of the novel."

"You're writing a novel about his life, yet that won't include our private lives? That doesn't sound convincing."

Suddenly Mona said, "You don't know anything about our lives. You hear things from Dad and he simply portrays them in his own way and you take that as the truth."

I had to admit to myself that that might be the case.

"He has so many deluded ideas and suspicions, and that's what has ruined our relationship," Awatef said. "Like once, when he heard some silly remark in a *diwaniya*! That's not my fault. Do I have to abandon my family to please him? He married me knowing we are different."

"He's the cause of the problem," Mona said. Awatef looked at her.

"I'm sick of this," Awatef continued. "We've spoken repeatedly about it, but he refuses to listen. Naturally, there's often a disparity between people. He is Khalid, and my father is Abdul Razzaq Al-Abdullatif. God created people on different levels. If Khalid refuses to accept that, then it's his problem." She looked at me directly. "Please keep out of this."

"Mr. Khalifa wants to write a novel about his experiences as a businessman."

"Mai clearly said you're going to write a novel about our father's life," Mona interjected. "Write about yourself as much as you like, but don't write about others."

I looked directly at Awatef. "Khalid signed a contract with me," I said.

"His name is Mr. Khalifa," Awatef said sharply. "Don't get carried away. He is not your close friend. No one in Kuwait has ever done what you and my husband want to do. Every society has its traditions, traditions that we have to respect."

"What you're saying has nothing to do with my agreement with Mr. Khalifa," I insisted.

"Of course it does! As in all Arab communities, our society will grab onto the tiniest morsel of gossip and rumor. If they don't read the words they want to find, they will simply read between the lines. Or even make up what they want to read. Khalid's novel will make me and my family the talk of the city. Whether you intend it or not, it will depict our relationship, or a version of it, and lay things bare that no one wants to have discussed or exposed. And worse, it'll damage the reputation of my children and will bring back to life a story that has slowly died over thirty years. More suffering because of a failed marriage. Would you want to live through that again? Your novel will open the gates of hell for us!"

"I understand what you're saying, but I believe you're exaggerating things and the possible effects."

"Oh you do, do you? You do not have the right to go into my house during my absence. I forbid it."

"I went into the house at Mr. Khalifa's request."

"That is my house, not Khalid's. I will not allow you to abuse it."

"There is no abuse."

"My husband is unwell, in both his feelings and his thinking, and he doesn't know what he's really doing. He wants to write a book about his business experiences. What, does he imagine himself an Onassis or a Rockefeller?!"

"My mother will reimburse you for the full amount of your contract," Mona said, spitting out the words. "Here is a check for the full amount."

I decided it was time for me to go. "I'm sorry, I have to leave," I said. "As I told your secretary, I unfortunately have another meeting."

"We must resolve this before you leave," Awatef insisted.

"I don't see there is anything left to discuss."

"I'm asking that we resolve this now. My family and I will not allow any writer to tarnish our reputation. Perhaps I ought to mention that it was supposed to be my brother Mubarak attending the meeting today. Can I tell you something in confidence?"

I nodded.

"A year ago, I asked Khalid for a divorce. He refused. Now he's taking revenge on me."

"My sister Mai said that you've been meeting with Dad

regularly," said Mona, "and that you're going to write about everything."

I shook my head. "I will write only what your father wants," I said.

"You won't write anything," said Awatef, offering me the check. "Take it and we're done."

"Unfortunately, money can't always resolve differences," I retorted.

"Some people don't want the Abdullatif family to prosper. There are hidden conflicts you don't know about. This is our battle. Why do you insist on being part of it?"

She looked at me and a moment of silence passed.

"I'm sorry," I said. "I signed a contract in good faith and I must fulfill it."

"We'll find a way to cancel the contract."

"Again, I regret I have to leave."

"I'm prepared to raise the amount …"

"Thanks, but no."

"I will not allow you to enter my house again!" Awatef shouted. "I will not allow you to write this!"

"Look," said Mona, "my mother would be prepared to raise the amount to 150,000."

That's more than half a million dollars, I said to myself in amazement.

"I will stop you writing by force of law if I must," Awatef said.

"Well, I have a legal contract, so I won't argue about resorting to the law."

The hatred that Awatef and her daughter exuded was palpable. In fact, I felt like everything in the office was trying to drive me away.

I thought that perhaps it really was time to leave. It didn't seem likely that we would reach any understanding. "Thank you for the meeting," I said as I began to rise.

"Wait! *I* asked for this meeting and *I* decide when it ends," said Awatef. I hesitated, though already on my feet and about to leave, and decided to let the angry woman have her last say.

"Alright. But not for too much longer," I conceded.

Suddenly the door opened, and in came Mai, of all the unexpected people.

"Good evening," she greeted me shyly. "Good evening, Mama."

I was glad I had stayed, though I now had doubts about Mai's role in the drama.

"I asked Mai to come," Awatef told me. "Unfortunately my beloved elder daughter here is not loyal to the secrets of her family. She even put the idea of writing this wretched novel into her father's head."

Mai just stood there embarrassed, then finally took a seat.

"You think you know everything about your father, Mai, but you don't," Awatef said, picking up a file from her desk. "This is something I have never shown you. I didn't want you to feel bad. I know how attached you are to your father and always have been. But ..." She handed the file to Mona, who was still standing next to her. "Give this to your sister and let her read the report the psychologist wrote about her beloved father."

Mai looked apprehensive.

I felt I ought to defend her in some way. "Mrs. Awatef," I said, "it seems it's actually you who's divulging secrets. Is this fair to your daughters?"

"Do not interfere with family matters!" snapped Awatef, turning again to Mai. "Your father is a psychopath, you see? He has an inferiority complex. It's there in the summary in the first paragraph. It's not my fault that he was the son of a poor civil servant and that he can't get over it."

"Mama, please …" Mai pleaded. "It's not right to speak like this about my father."

"I agree," I said. "And this is none of my business. So if our business is concluded …" I got up again.

"Before you go, don't you want to know about the illness of your novel's hero?" Awatef said with derision. "Khalid has been diagnosed as a psychopath. He has obsessions and strange ideas. He believes that society despises his achievements, that his peers look down on him, and that even I treat him unfairly. He's obsessed with the idea that people know my father made him what he is. And he refuses to see how my family is behind his success."

"Whether you leave or not, you can be sure of this: we will *not* allow you to write a novel about my father," Mona said.

"Who said I'm waiting for your permission?" I retorted. "I don't recall seeing your name on the contract I signed with your father."

"Don't you *dare* speak to my daughter in that tone!" Awatef shouted.

"Nor, for that matter, your name either, Mrs. Awatef," I added.

"For the last time, I warn you!" said Awatef, glowering at me. When I didn't rise to the bait, she added, "Tell the hero of your novel that he needs to make peace with himself. And entertain himself. He is a millionaire and he can live as he chooses but *not* when it dishonors my family."

"Good day to you both," I said. "And to you, Mai. I'll see you later, I hope." I moved toward the door.

"You will *not* see her and I will not let her meet you. I will call the police if you dare enter my house again."

I reached the door, with Awatef's voice following me. I turned to face her. Our eyes met briefly before I turned away and closed the door behind me. How on earth did you get yourself into this crazy situation? I asked myself.

Chapter 9

Tuesday, May 8, 2007

I had no idea how things had become so complicated. The moment I left Awatef's office, Shoroq called me, asking me about the meeting.

"If I said it was bad, I'd be lying," I told her. "It was beyond bad. It was awful."

"What happened?"

"I'll explain later."

After lunch, I told her the whole story while she played with Fadia.

"What'll you do now?"

I shrugged my shoulders. "Think about it, I suppose." I took Fadia into my lap and picked up one of her favorite dolls. "She's a bit of a mess, isn't she? Let's straighten her up a little, shall we?" I said.

Fadia began to pull at the doll's clothes, straightening her outfit and preening her hair with her fingers, talking to her.

"You ought to tell Mr. Khalifa," Shoroq said. "The relationship is with him. Awatef has no right to interfere."

I was reluctant to rush into a decision. Who knew, maybe I could get out of writing the book and make a good deal of money at the same time.

"I'm wondering, though," Shoroq continued.

"Yes?"

"Well, if you take Awatef's offer, it might be a trap to implicate him or something?"

"I don't know," I admitted. Trap him? Implicate him? It sounded like some crazy soap opera with a plot that no one would believe.

"On the other hand, we would still receive the same amount as compensation," Shoroq continued, thinking aloud.

"I can't break a contract so easily," I said with a sigh. "I think I'll go and sleep on it a little."

I tried to sleep but found it impossible. So I decided to call my lawyer. I told him about my meeting with Awatef.

"You need to be careful," he advised. "Mrs. Awatef would have the right to sue you if the novel damaged her reputation in any way or affected her relationship with her husband or family. If you're going to mention people by their real names, you'll be stepping into a minefield."

I was anxious now. Should I tell Khalid about the meeting? I'd already spent the first payment. And how was I going to visit him at home? Awatef had told me clearly that the house was hers, not his.

I decided to visit my writer friend, Ismail Fahad, and take his advice.

"How's the novel?" he asked, as he always did.

"How is it? Convoluted!" I told him. "Yesterday I met Khalid's wife."

He smiled. "Good for you."

"She told me to stop writing, and basically threatened me if I published the novel. And she offered me 150,000 dinars."

"Really? Take the money and stop writing immediately!" he said with the same smile. "No Arab writer ever makes that kind of money! Why does she want you to stop writing it?"

"She said she wants to avoid gossip and scandal. She's convinced that, even though I told her that Khalid wants no mention of personal or family details, readers will read things into it and make things up."

"What did her husband say about you meeting her?"

"I haven't told him. At least, not yet. I'm rather at a loss as to what to do."

Ismail thought for a moment, lit a cigarette and took a deep breath.

"Tell me, what do you make of the man?" he asked.

"He's a simple and honest man, but someone who has been through a good deal of suffering unfortunately."

"Well, if the man is honest, then you should fulfill the contract and let Mrs. Awatef go to hell, I say!"

"So you're in favor of me completing the novel?"

"Sure. Continue your meetings with the man and write your novel."

On Ismail's advice, I made my decision. I would write the novel. And I decided to tell Khalid about my meeting with his wife. I called him to do so less than half an hour later.

"Good evening," he said in a tired tone.

"I'm calling to see how you are."

"I'm fine, thank you."

"I met Mrs. Awatef."

There was a pause before he replied: "I'd rather you told me about that in person."

"I'm afraid it's going to be difficult for me to go there now," I said.

"I'll be waiting for you, I want to know." He paused to catch his breath with difficulty. "Please don't delay. Please, this is a personal request, Taleb."

"OK, see you at six o'clock."

Next time, I'll invite him to my house, I thought. And maybe I'd meet with Mai once or twice since she was closest to him.

As on the previous occasion, Khalid's house was quiet when I arrived. Awatef had warned me not to go into her house, so I couldn't help but hesitate. And no one was waiting for me this time, I noticed.

This 100,000 dinars isn't going to come easy, I thought.

A female voice called down to me. "Hello! Come right in!"

Though I couldn't tell for sure, I expected it was Mai. I went in and walked through the hall into the elevator. The place reeked of the usual distinctive incense. The whole place evoked silence and loneliness. The elevator door opened and I heard Khalid's voice greeting me.

He looked tired. He was in a *dishdasha*, his head uncovered as usual. We shook hands and he led me to where we had sat in front of the TV the previous time.

"So tell me, why didn't you want to come here?" he asked.

Awatef looked at me from out of the picture frame. "Oh, I didn't want to trouble you," I replied.

"It's OK. Please don't shy away from answering."

"I met Mrs. Awatef yesterday," I said.

"She asked to meet you?"

"Yes."

"What did she want from you?"

"She told me to stop writing the novel."

"By what right does she tell you that?"

"She's worried the novel will damage her reputation and that of her family."

Khalid appeared to be having some difficulty breathing. "Did you explain to her that it's about my experiences that you're going to write and that I'll read it before publication?"

Mai came in, carrying a small tea tray. "Good evening," she said. I noticed a shade of sorrow on her face. "So, how are Shoroq and Fadia?"

"Fine, thank you. They are waiting for you to visit."

"I'm committed to the contract between us," I told Khalid.

"You won't go back on your word?"

"Nothing would persuade me to go back on my word."

"Mona told Mai that her mother offered you 150,000 dinars and you refused because you wanted more."

I was shocked and suddenly found myself on the defensive.

"That is not true," I said. "I refused because I'm committed to writing the novel unless you change your mind."

Suddenly, the elevator door opened and a woman strode out. Now we're in trouble, I thought. Awatef marched over toward us, with Mona in tow.

Mai got up, though I noticed that Khalid remained seated.

"We were passing by the house and Mona saw your car," Awatef told me angrily, her eyes shooting sparks. Khalid invited her to take a seat but she ignored him and addressed me again.

"I asked you not to enter my house," she said.

"I called and asked Taleb to come to my house," Khalid interjected. "You can sit with us."

"I don't want to sit with him. He will leave my house immediately."

It was like a slap in the face. I stood up to leave, but Khalid urged me to stay.

"Please sit. You are a guest in my house," he said. Then, turning to Awatef, he continued, "I'm going to talk with Taleb for a while. You can wait for me if you like. Sit with the girls until we're done here."

"Don't expose our family secrets to someone who'll use them to his own benefit!" shouted Awatef.

"Mrs. Awatef," I said.

"Please," Khalid said to me, and to his wife, "Enough is enough."

"It will be enough when you stop this stupid project!"

"Please, Mr. Khalid, I should go."

"No. Please sit, I want to talk to you."

I felt embarrassed and didn't know what to do.

Khalid's face was contorted with barely controlled anger. "Please leave us alone for now," he said to his wife.

"You want to punish me because I asked for a divorce. Is that it?"

"No, that's just what your twisted mind is telling you."

"Anyone who tries to stain my reputation will pay a dear price! And I mean you!" she said, looking at me. "I will make you regret every word you ever write."

"You're threatening us?" Khalid asked.

"If you go through with this book, you will be defying me and my family." I noticed she was trembling. "Come to your senses and don't forget the favors my father did for you. Don't malign those who helped you. Abdul Razzaq made you from nothing."

"How did I know you would say that?" Khalid said with a sigh.

"All Kuwaitis know your story! If you're seeking revenge on us, my family and I will be stronger than you. And we know how to stop you. I know," she added, then turned and marched off toward the elevator.

In the sudden calm all I could hear was Khalid's heavy breathing.

"You see?" he said, struggling for his next breath.

"Please, try to calm down," I said, handing him a glass of water.

"See how I suffer," he croaked.

Awatef's voice came to us from somewhere else in the house. She seemed to be shouting at Mai.

"Since we got married," Khalid continued, "I've wanted to stand beside her on her level, but she insisted on standing alone. What bothers me the most is how she claims some kind of position for herself simply by being the daughter of Abdul Razzaq. That and how she never misses an opportunity to remind me of her father's help."

He sat back against the bench. "Love between men and women is a third creature formed from the two. It might be warm or cruel. It lives between them and carries the makeup of each. Love has that frightening ability to turn against lovers. It torments them, knowing their weak points."

He looked up at me and I felt embarrassed, though a part of me could see the literary possibilities of the drama.

"I sentenced myself to a life of humiliation the moment I married Awatef. For a while I felt proud to be the husband of Abdul Razzaq's daughter, but soon I understood that if you want to wear gold, there's a price. It was the gamble of my life … but it was a gamble I lost. The clothes I was expected to wear didn't fit. They were simply too big for me and I kept stumbling. It's very difficult for a man to live with a woman who makes him feel she is condescending to him. How can a man live in a society that does not respect his dignity?"

He paused, apparently relieved to have lifted a weight off his chest. I didn't know if I should stay or leave.

"Would you like some orange juice?" asked Mai, speaking from nowhere.

"I'm sorry," said Khalid. "I never thought this novel would cause so much trouble."

"Take it easy, Dad," said Mai.

"But we will finish the novel together," Khalid said, turning to me.

"Sure," I said, getting up. I walked toward the elevator, feeling like I was running away.

As I walked to my car, it felt like the garden too was fearful, and I imagined I could hear Awatef's voice following me: "I'm watching you …"

Chapter 10

Thursday, May 10, 2007

Before I went to sleep, Farah called.

"It is twelve o'clock and one second. Happy birthday!" she shouted down the phone.

I laughed. I had forgotten my own birthday.

"Sweetie, I don't care for birthday celebrations," I said.

"But I care, even if I have to celebrate your birthday alone."

After I finished the call, Shoroq kissed me and whispered, "How old are you now?"

I smiled at her. "Oh, I don't know. Anyway, new novel, new me."

A lovely smile lit up her face and she hugged me.

The meeting with Khalid and his wife had thrown me into confusion about the novel, but later I sat in my office to start writing. I went over all the notes I had written and, as I was doing so, an idea came to me: I would divide the novel into chapters according to the real events that had happened. Buoyed, I started the first chapter.

Chapter 1

Wednesday, March 28, 2007

It was half past two in the afternoon. Exhausted, I was driving home along Morocco

Highway, annoyed by the snarled traffic. My mobile rang. I didn't recognize the number.

"Hello?" I said.

"Taleb Alrefai?" a woman's soft voice asked.

"Yes," I replied.

"Good afternoon."

"And the same to you."

"This is Khalid Khalifa's office calling."

I was busy writing when my phone rang.

"Good evening," a rough voice announced. "I am Mubarak Al-Abdullatif."

"Good evening."

"Perhaps you know the reason why I'm calling? My sister Awatef has told me about the book you're writing. We had hoped to find an amicable solution."

Just like his sister, I thought.

"I know you met in her office and I know she offered you excellent compensation."

I chose to stay silent.

"Unfortunately, you didn't respect her offer or her wishes, and you again went to her house, even though she had warned you not to. Which is why I'm calling you."

He may have expected to hear a reply, but I remained silent.

"I hope you will now cease going to her house and have finished with this book business." His tone sounded more threatening.

"I don't know whether Mrs. Awatef has told you about the contract between me and Mr. Khalid?" I asked.

"I do not care about the contract, nor about Khalid. And I wonder why a Kuwaiti writer such as yourself would wish to slander a well-known Kuwaiti family such as ours."

"There's no question of slander," I protested.

"You're writing about my sister, about her relationship with her husband, and about our father and you say there's no slander? Rubbish! People's private lives must be respected and remain protected. That crazy Khalid tempted you with a silly amount of money and you agreed to write for him. That's not the attitude of a decent writer. I'm sure you know about the Abdullatif family. So, I ask you again. Walk away from this book. Our compensation offer is still on the table."

"Excuse me," I finally said. "I get the message."

"Can we consider this to be over?"

"Yes, this call can be considered to be over."

A pause. "Am I to understand that you don't wish to cooperate with us?"

"Thanks," I said and ended the call.

After Mubarak's call, I spent my evening annoyed and went to bed upset. I dreamed a tangle of dreams. I saw people carrying Khalid on their shoulders. He was asleep, stock still, on an old piece of wood. They walked toward the sea. My mother was sitting on the seashore near Awatef and Mona. The moment the people approached the sea, Khalid got up and jumped into the water.

The next morning, while I was sitting in my office at the National Council, Mai called me.

"Good morning," she said. "My … my father's in the hospital."

I was shocked and said I hoped it wasn't serious.

"It … was a-a heart attack," she said, and started to sob. "Why did this happen …?"

"Where is your father now?"

"In the Amiri Hospital."

"Can I visit him?"

"He's not allowed visitors. He, he's in the intensive care unit now," she sniffled. "I'm arranging his medical reports in order for Mom and me to take him to London."

"Your mom?"

"Yes."

"May God help him and I hope everything turns out well," I said.

"I-I'm scared," she said, sniffing back her tears. "I mean, what if he …?"

I wanted to console her but all I could say was, "Try not to trouble yourself with bad thoughts."

When she ended the call, I felt like I had been dropped into a void. Two months earlier I hadn't known Khalid Khalifa, except through his pictures in the newspapers. I would never have imagined us having a relationship. Yet Mai's call made me feel like a family friend. A friend from whom Mai was looking for help. She had said she would travel with her mother to move her father to London.

I wondered why Awatef had decided to go to London with Khalid. Had there been some kind of reconciliation?

I called Shoroq and told her the news. "Oh, and Awatef and her brother threatened me," I added.

"Please, let this novel go. You're no match for the Abdullatif family. And nothing good has come of this."

It had just been my birthday and suddenly I found myself in a dilemma: Should I start off my new year by writing this troubled novel?

***

Later, I sat alone in front of my computer. The house was quiet. Fadia was asleep and Shoroq was watching a movie.

After dinner, I had told her I needed to sit by myself for a while.

She had looked at me. Despite all the years we had spent together, she still didn't understand how I needed to be alone when I was upset.

I needed my friend, silence, to help me make decisions.

I had had five meetings with Khalid and he had opened his heart to me. After Awatef threatened me, he still insisted on writing the novel.

I could not publish the novel before Khalid read it – that was part of the contract. I had received the first installment of 20,000 dinars. And I needed the rest of it.

Khalid had fallen ill and I had to wait. Well, my life had always been a series of waiting.

Now that Khalid was ill, Awatef wanted to be by his side. I reminded myself that there was a big difference between love and compassion.

I had rejected her silly offer and then she said I'd blackmailed her. What might she do next? I wondered.

I thought perhaps the time to start writing had come. I had plenty of material, some in notes on my computer and some in my head. Ideally I needed to have more meetings with Khalid but there was the possibility that he might not survive. Then there was the paragraph in the contract that gave me the right to the full amount if Khalid failed to give me the information I needed.

It would be very difficult to write about Khalid without bringing in his personal history, his marriage, and his relationship with the Abdullatif family. But he had told me he wanted the Kuwaiti people to know his life story.

"Oil never mixes with water," he said.

But Awatef had been equally adamant when she told me not to write about the secrets of powerful, well-known families like hers.

I sighed. For a year I had been looking for an idea for a novel, and now I had one. Khalid's story was worth telling, even if I had to wait for Khalid to recover. Then I would write the novel. I would not let it die.

The threats from Awatef and her brother would not frighten me off. No one would make me abandon writing this novel. Time had taught me that writing was a risk-taking process from beginning to end.

Just go ahead and write, I told myself. There's no need to wait.

Then I realized that the book had written itself, and here it is.